Vacation Deadly

An Action-Adventure Thriller Collection

Kat Simons

Vacation Deadly

Contents

To my hero and our heroes in training.

Introduction

I have always loved a good action-adventure movie. Add in a little humor and I'm all in. The more over the top, the better. I grew up watching the action-adventure thrillers of the 80s and still love a good larger-than-life hero. *Die Hard, Aliens, True Lies, Demolition Man, Indiana Jones, Jumanji, Laura Kroft, Jurassic Park.* It's got adventure, travel, action, fun characters, and a bit of a laugh in the middle of all the gunfights... I love it.

And sometimes, I even commit action-adventure thriller while writing.

Travel is also a big part of my life. As a mother, the idea of a quiet holiday on a beach with plenty of time to read is...a dream. But traveling with my kids is great fun, too. And who doesn't love a nice little get away, quiet, no one to bother you, nothing to do but kick back and enjoy yourself…

Unfortunately, when your real life is as complicated as the main characters in this collection, a little quiet time is never really on the table. In fact, sometimes a vacation can turn deadly.

VACATION DEADLY includes five all new action-adventure thrillers, with main characters that take life by the throat and go all in. As you might be able to tell, I have a soft spot for thieves, but also the occasional assassin. Sometimes, though, I just like a larger-than-life type of character willing to go in and do the thing because it's the right thing to do.

I have a little of all that here.

The first story, *Blue Skies and Conman's Eyes*, jumps right into the theme of this collection with a main character just looking for a break on her all-you-can-eat cruise around the Hawaiian Islands. But her reputation follows her. Some people just can't get away from work.

And speaking of not being able to get away from work! In *A Vacation to Die For*, our heroine goes all the way to a tiny island off the coast of Bali just for a little quite reading time. But no. Work has to call. And… Well, let's just say, destroying an assassin's book before she's finished reading it is a bad idea. Very bad.

In *Darwin's Atoll*, our main characters end up

exactly where they want to be, just not with the people they wanted along for the ride. They probably should have checked who owned that yacht. Treasure hunting does have its drawbacks, even in the tropics.

Taking the Heat takes a little turn, heading into the mountains, with a main character whose past has left her avoiding the thing she loves most. But when push comes to shove, and people are in need, she does what she has to do. And maybe along the way can find some forgiveness for herself.

Finally, the collection ends in the great outdoors with *Deadly Breaks*. More beautiful mountain scenery and clean, pine-scented air. All of which the main character hates. The moose doesn't help. He hates the open air and beautiful forest even more when the bullets start flying.

This collection is full of fun adventure stories with a thriller twist that I hope will keep readers entertained. I know they sure kept me entertained when I was writing them.

Thanks for picking up VACATION DEADLY! I hope you enjoy it.

Kat Simons
May 2024

Blue Skies and Conman's Eyes

1

My first holiday in five years, and I'd been looking forward to that break like you wouldn't believe. No idea why I expected it to be anything but a disaster. My life is one big walking disaster after another. But I had some "Love Boat" crap in my head. My dad played that show constantly when I was a kid, always on in the background. It stuck in deep. I thought a cruise around the Hawaiian Islands would be my Love Boat.

Boy, was I wrong.

The crowds at the dock where thick and pushy, half of them dressed in cheap, scratchy Hawaiian shirts. A handful had picked up the good stuff and were wearing nice, authentic Hawaiian shirts. Still, it was a lot of flowers on a lot of well-fed white people. I did like the flower lei they handed out before boarding. Smelled like the islands. Like heaven as far as I was concerned. The air was hot and damp, but the breeze was nice when it broke through the crowds.

"That breeze'll feel great at sea, eh?" This from one of the tourists crowded up next to me, a middle aged white guy I gave a passing glance.

"Sure," I said, forcing a smile.

Not sure why I was trying to be friendly. Not like I intended on spending much time with any of these people. I was here for the drink card, the all you could eat buffet, and the spa. Maybe a little touristing on the islands when we stopped, but not with groups. I was sick up to my eyeballs of people. Any people.

So why, you might ask, was I cruising—stuck on a giant floating city with a bunch of people intent on getting drunk and stuffing their faces and spending over the top for knock off Coach bags? I could have gone to a secluded island in east Asia and hidden in a cabana on the sea with no internet and few people and just the ocean and the sun as my company.

Sounds nice until you *have* to do it. Been there, done that. Got the t-shirt. Wasn't my cup of tea, as they say.

Anyway, the crowds pushed and shoved through all the security, up the gangway to the main deck. Lots of laughing and too-loud talking. Lots of crew directing everyone around, checking boarding tickets. They took our luggage before boarding, promising it would be in our rooms when we got there. Fine by me. I'd overpacked a little. I might want to spend all my time in the spa or eating, but I intended to do it in style since I didn't have to lug the suitcase around between destinations. Love Boat illusions and pretty sandals. That was my goal.

I was apparently not the only one who packed this way for the cruise. The number of oversized luggage that, from the way the crew hefted it, had to be filled with bricks, was more than a little awe-inspiring.

Plenty of crew around onboard too, making sure we all got to the right elevators and the right floors to find our rooms. I'd sprung for an outside room so I'd have a window, but nothing with a balcony cause I'd stay up all night imagining falling off that balcony into the Pacific Ocean and never being seen again. I'm a good swimmer. Kind of have to be. But I doubted my ability to survive the Pacific long enough to reach land.

I felt for the people in the interior rooms, with no windows, but I figured the ones booking those rooms only meant to sleep in them and maybe have sex but otherwise would spend most of their time by the pool or in the restaurants and bars and stuff. I spotted one of those interior rooms when I was hunting down mine, and… Yeah, they weren't gonna be spending much time in those cramped and lightless spaces.

My room, when I finally reached it after going up

and down amazingly long corridors, was bright, comfortably sized for a single traveler—not too big, not too small—and had a bathroom I wouldn't have to turn sideways to get through the door.

As this was my first time on a cruise, I really hadn't known what to expect, but based on all the trains and planes I've been on over the years, I was impressed by the bathroom.

There was a towel on the bed folded into a swan, which was cute, and my suitcase was already waiting for me. That was some backdoor process. I made a mental note to figure out how my suitcase made it here so fast—old habits, looking for the quickest way out, etc… Though where the hell I thought I'd go in the middle of the Pacific, I had no idea.

I stepped to the window, admired the less than scenic view of the docks, substantially less crowded than before. The warehouses from this angle looked a little less beat up. The big tour group buses that had crowded the parking lot across from the dock had thinned out. Beyond the docks, though, the fern and tree-covered volcanic mountains rose to dominate the background. A lot prettier than the dark stained buildings and cement surrounding the docks. Hell of a lot prettier than New York.

Still not entirely sure why I choose Hawaii for this cruise, with the required eleven hour flight to get here, instead of the Caribbean. Guess, I figured I'd be less likely to run into anyone I knew. Which was part of the point of a vacation for me.

I wanted to unpack my suitcase but I was also starving and wanted to scout out the restaurants and bars and most especially the spa. I was ready for a week of spa treatments. I'd never indulged in spa treatments. Like I said, delusions of Love Boat, though in my case, I wasn't interested in the "love" part. Just the boat.

Ignoring my suitcase, I made my way through the labyrinthine corridors—which you'd think would be straight forward, up and down the length of the boat, but for reasons surpassing logic, there were a lot of corridors wrapping around each other. At least it felt that way. I needed a map. There'd probably been one in my room, but I didn't want to hike back to find it. When I finally spotted one posted on the walls, that helped clear things up. I suspected I wasn't the only one who got turned around.

Did an about face and headed in the right direction to reach the pool deck and the big buffet. There was a vibration in the floor, the engines on and churning, but that had been there even while we were docked, so I didn't realize we'd moved out to sea until I stepped out to the poolside and spotted the island mountains a significantly farther distance away. I couldn't feel the giant ship moving. The only reason I knew we were was because the island was moving past. That was impressive. Probably helped with motion sickness for those who suffered. I was lucky. Stomach like steal. But I liked I wouldn't feel the ship rocking. That kind of thing brought bad memories.

Bumped into a few people on my way to the buffet, including the middle aged white guy who'd tried to talk to me down on the dock. He waved like we were old friends. "How you like your room? Mine's nice. Little swan on the bed. I love that. This your first cruise?"

"No," I lied with a straight face. "But first time on a ship this big." Which was enough truth to keep me honest—ha!—and also keep me from looking stupid when I got lost and, of course, this guy would be the one to spot me and direct me.

Since he was pretending we knew each other, I took a minute to study him a bit closer. Middle aged white guy impression didn't change much. He wore one of the better Hawaiian shirts, muted flowers in blue and white, and tan pocketed shorts. His blondish-brown hair was going gray, but it blended in well with the base color. He was darkly tanned, unlike my pale white New Yorker complexion, though I couldn't tell if it was real or fake—so if it was fake, it was a great job—and he had the kind of comfortable face that could be overlooked in a crowd.

I made an effort to be overlooked in a crowd most of the time, too. Which was why I was dressed in shorts and a t-shirt with a giant red Hibiscus on the front. My brown hair was pulled back into a lazy ponytail. My black flipflops had been purchased at a tourist store in Waikiki where the clerk called them slippers. I had embraced the tourist look as completely as I could tolerate. Though I kept my glasses on instead of indulging in contacts. I hated contacts. I wore them when I had to, when I was working, but this was supposed to be a vacation, not work.

Supposed to be.

I tried to smile and move around the guy, but he followed me to the buffet, chatting away about the drinks card, free food, and the first tour he was taking when we reached Kauai, the first stop on the cruise. I sure hoped this guy didn't think I was going to be his Love Boat experience. People like me, we don't do relationships if we can avoid them. Too much to lose if you have a close relationship of some kind. Too many chances of being caught flat-footed and someone gets hurt. Might even die.

I considered making excuses and ditching him. I wanted to eat all the food in peace. There was a lot of it and I intended on sampling everything then going back for the good things until I was good and stuffed. Then a nap—alone!—in my room. Then I'd unpack. Putting the unpacking off felt rebellious. Hell, yeah, I was on a vacation. I don't have to unpack until I'm damned good and ready.

That'll teach me. Should have unpacked the minute I got aboard.

The chatty guy stayed in line with me as we filled plates. Then followed me to a seat near a window looking out over the sea. This deck was high and gave excellent views of rolling blue water and blue blue skies. I kept my attention on the view as chatty guy went on and on about his business selling real estate in California. Suppose that explained the tan. Only good thing about his company was he didn't require much from me. Didn't ask questions that would require more lies. Didn't even ask my name. Spent the whole time talking about himself and I was more than content to let him so long as I got a second serving of pineapple ice cream because that shit was good.

When I couldn't fit in anymore food or ice cream, I tried to make my excuses. "Need a nap now," I said with a half laugh.

"I'll walk you back," he said. "I got lost finding my room. This place is a labyrinth. Better to have someone with you if you get lost, right? Company until you find your way around. This isn't my first cruise, either, but still I got lost. I love these things. I cruise all the time. Love the sea breeze."

Since I couldn't get a word in to politely refuse his company back to my room, I slogged on, counting the minutes until I could ditch this guy. I didn't want to make a scene. I didn't want to call attention to myself.

That was the whole point. No reason to pick me out of the crowd on a cruise ship full of pasty or artificially tanned tourists. You'd be surprised by how many people notice you when you're making an effort to be alone. No one looks twice when you're one of many in a crowd.

At least that's been my experience.

The chatty guy followed me all the way to my room before finally giving me a little salute and continuing on down the corridor. "One floor down, same side of the ship," he said. "Great coincidence, huh?"

"Sure," I said with my forced smile and made sure he'd vanished into the labyrinth before I went into my room and locked the door behind me. Paranoia was a hazard of the job. I saw no reason to ditch that on this vacation even though I'd ditched most all of my other work-related habits.

Okay, well, not all of them.

Couldn't get a gun on a cruise ship. Lot of metal detectors and scanners getting through the docks and onto the ship, all the luggage scanned. I was good with that. I hated guns, even though I occasionally had call to use them. But I didn't like traveling without any weapons at all, even on vacation. Night sticks and batons aren't allowed on the cruise either. But I've got a big, thick wooden stick that I've covered in detailed, anatomically correct—if exaggerated—plastic, so when scanned or when some noisy inspector looks closely at my stuff, all they see is a dildo. A rather impressive one, too. No one questions the purpose of a dildo. Everyone knows what they're for.

After another look out my window, at the now significantly prettier view of the Pacific, I turned to my suitcase.

And realized with no little alarm that it wasn't mine.

Great. Just great. Now I had to go to all the trouble of sorting out missing luggage. But at least it would be on the ship somewhere. I hoped my suitcase hadn't been left behind. I didn't want to spend that much money replacing my wardrobe. And I'd be sorry to lose my baton disguised as a dildo. Lot of work went into getting that just right.

I plunked the case up on my bed, squashing the towel swan, mores the pity, and checked the tag.

Uh…?

Tag had my name on it, well the name I was using for the cruise, the name on all my current IDs. But this was definitely not my bag.

No lock, so I opened it. Inside, full of women's clothing, my sizes, nothing I would have actually bought for myself, though. Lot of sparkles. I'm not a sparkles person. I don't mind a nice high heel every so often, when warranted. But sparkles? In the heat? No.

Even the swimsuit was covered in sequins. Who the hell wore sequins in the pool?

I stared down into the case, hands on hips, wondering what the hell was going on.

A knock on the door.

I looked up. Shit. I really should have known I couldn't just take a normal vacation.

2

That the person on the other end of the knock was the middle aged white guy who'd been clinging to me was not surprising. That he was holding a gun pointed at me was.

"How'd you get that thing through all the security?" I asked.

"Friend on the security team. Little bribery. Same way I got that suitcase delivered to your room."

"What happened to my real luggage?" I'd put a lot of work into that dildo club so it would get through security scans and x-ray machines. I'd hate to lose it. Had a few pairs of cute vacation sandals I would hate to lose, too.

"I've got that, don't worry. And if you cooperate, no one needs to know about any of this. Nice dildo in there, by the way."

"I like it."

"Kind of big."

"Depends on your perspective."

"You going to let me in or not."

"Considering it. Why do I care if anyone knows I got the wrong luggage?"

"Lots of stolen jewels in the liner to send you up for…oh, for a while. You've managed to avoid jail for a long time… What is it on this trip? Beth Harold? Beth?"

"Short for Elizabeth. Mom named me after the queen. Real anglophile."

"Good story. Beth." He smiled as he repeated my fake name. Then waved the gun a little. "Let's go inside and talk. I could only get my friend in security to tamper with the corridor cameras for so long."

"I could just keep you standing here until someone notices you holding a gun."

"And then I'd make sure they searched your bag. You don't think I've got a backup plan? You think I'm new to this?"

"Depends on what this is."

"Inside, Beth. We got some things to discuss."

Letting this guy into my room was not a good idea. Letting him frame me for theft was even worse. Unfortunately, I didn't know whether he was bluffing or not because I hadn't had time to go through the bag yet. Should have choose "unpack bag" over "buffet" as first things first. Live and learn.

Since, so far, he was being reasonable and also he had a gun, I stepped aside and let him in. I closed the door, mostly, as he walked to the window and looked out. Shame I didn't have a balcony. I could have pushed him off. Although, I still hadn't heard what all this was about, so probably should get to that first before dumping him into the ocean.

"You're really good," he said. "I've been following your career for the last ten years. Really good."

"How do you know who I am and I don't know you?"

"You don't know me because I haven't worked on the east coast in…twenty-five, thirty years."

"You don't look old enough for that sentence."

"Thanks." He flashed me a smile over his shoulder, then turned to face me, the gun pointing at me again. "The plastic surgeons in California are excellent."

"Yeah they are. Well done."

"How old are you now? Twenty-eight, thirty?"

"Thirty-six."

"You look good, too. Surgery?"

"Good genes."

"Until they aren't. Trust me. Surgery will be your friend one day."

"Are you kidding me? All the magazines tell me I'm gonna be invisible when I hit fifty. That's what happens to women apparently. Surgery hell. I get to be invisible, I'm gonna rob banks."

He chuckled. "Career change that late in life is hard."

"Speaking from experience?"

"Me? No. I've always been a conman. Will be to the day I die. Loved that job you did in Thailand, by the way. Really slick."

I made a face. "That was kind of an accident." Another vacation gone wrong. You'd think I'd have learned my lesson after that. But the influence of "Love Boat" obviously overrode all common sense.

"You're the best con I've seen in years. Must say, I'm a little jealous."

"Can't be that good if you know who I am." And wasn't that just a blow to the ego. I'd taken great pains to ensure I looked exactly like every other tourist on this ship. And still got made by another con artist. Maybe he wasn't wrong about the surgery if I was that easy to spot.

"Don't take it personally. I've been at this a long time. I keep up on all the people in our business, make it my business if you will."

"Great. What's this about?"

"I've got a job I need to bring to a finish. Here on this ship. And you're going to help me so the nice old woman I've been working has no idea what happened. We'll both get away with a small fortune—yes, I'll give you a cut. Ten percent? That's fair considering you're just coming in at the end. Ten percent of a fortune is still a fortune. But I need a younger woman who I can pass off as my niece, and I can't risk this game on an amateur."

"Why not just…approach me with the job?" I motioned to the suitcase. "Why all this?" I still wasn't convinced there was incriminating stolen items in the case, but I wasn't not convinced either. He went to all the trouble of getting a gun on board a cruise ship. Why half-ass the framing threat, right?

"You've got a reputation, Beth. Work alone. Double cross anyone dumb enough to work with you. They end up going down for the crimes if things go wrong. Can't have that."

"You think this approach is going to endear you to me?"

"No. But I do think it'll keep you honest. Remember my friend on the security team. He's getting five percent. He's got a vested interest in making sure I stay out of jail."

"How many percentages have you given away?" That's why I worked alone. I'm going to do all that work, I'm getting the bulk of the prize. A few one-time-only bribes were one thing. Percentage of the take? No way.

"Just you and my security friend. I've been working this one a long time. I've earned the pay day."

"Fair enough. What's the job?"

"Just like that?"

I sighed as I watched another vacation disintegrate. "I'm deciding if time in jail is better or worse than whatever you're offering. If what you're offering is better, I'll do it. I'd hate to break my streak of avoiding jail at all costs."

He smiled. The ordinary, middle aged white guy guise fell away then. The smile was cocky and just a little too smug. His expression calculating. Yeah. I'd seen that look before. So that's where we stood.

Good to know.

3

He'd been working the old lady for two long years, telling her tails of his niece and her budding charity organization. Helping kids with disabilities, first a horse riding place, now looking to expand to a swim-with-the-dolphins type thing. Gertrude Stemberger apparently had more money than god and a grandchild with Down syndrome, so she was ripe for the "disabled kids" charity con.

Rob York, as he was calling himself for this con, had never once asked Gertrude for a donation or contribution to his niece's charity. Rob did some real estate work for Gertrude, talked to her about the charity all the time. Never brought up donations.

It was a good ploy. All rich people expect other people to ask them for money. Especially for charities. At the least, they get invited to outrageously priced charity dinners and then asked for even more money for some worthy cause.

Gertrude was likely no exception, and being this side of eighty, she wasn't exactly new to the dance. She'd probably expected Rob to ask for money within days of bringing up his niece's charity. The fact that he'd gone for two years without doing so, two years of chatting about it and never once asking for money, would prime Gertrude to see his first request for a donation as "very important" and not something she had to be suspicious of.

Rob was good, too. He'd had a fake organization set up that Gertrude could investigate and find was both real and in good standing. He'd shown her pictures of his niece and the horses—doctored and always with a view of his niece that didn't show her face. He'd done all the things to ensure Gertrude trusted him and considered him a nice, honest businessman.

Apparently, Gertrude was now ripe for the plucking. His words, not mine.

The cruise was something she'd "talked him into" because he'd never been on one. He'd convinced her this one was the one to take. And she'd insisted he invite his niece.

At first, I thought that was his mistake, but turned out he'd picked this cruise because he knew I'd be on it. Long con. Should have known.

Gertrude was a nice old lady. Five foot nothing, wearing bright yellow slacks, pretty and orthopedically appropriate sandals, and a flowered blouse that fluttered in the breeze up on deck. She covered her gray hair with a huge brimmed yellow hat and sat in one of the lounge chairs like she owned the deck, sipping a martini, waving bejeweled hands around like there weren't thieves in her midst calculating the value of each and every ring on her fingers. One of the polite and chipper deck hands came around with more drinks, which Gertrude availed herself of, giving the young woman a wink as she slipped her a folded bill.

"Pays to keep the good will of the people bringing you drinks," she said when I raised my brows. "I believe in tipping generously."

"A good philosophy," I said, smiling my best "Rob's niece" smile.

I could see why he picked Gertrude for the con. At first blush, she was rich and generous and easy with her money. I wouldn't have targeted Gertrude, though. Not in a million years. Not because she was a nice old lady, or a generous tipper. That first blush impression didn't plumb the depths of character in the woman sitting casually under the ridiculously large hat sipping martinis surrounded by coconut-lotion smelling tourists.

I recognized an act when I saw one.

Apparently, Rob didn't. Which was interesting.

"I love the work you do, dear," Gertrude said. "Your uncle has told me all about it. Beautiful work. Beautiful."

"Thank you very much. The kids are worth all the hard work."

"They are, they are! He's told you I have a soft spot for your kind of work, hasn't he?"

"No." I glanced at my "uncle." "You never said anything like that."

"I have a grandson with Down syndrome, you see," Gertrude said. "Beautiful boy. So sweet. He also loves horses. Couldn't get him to swim with dolphins, I'm sure, but he loves horses. If he didn't live on the east coast, I'd probably see if you had room in your program for him."

"Oh, that's a shame. Maybe I could find something for him closer to home? I've met a lot of people doing really good work over the last few years. I'm sure someone is doing something similar closer to where he lives."

"Aren't you very good? What a sweetheart. Your uncle said you were a sweetheart, didn't you Rob. Such a sweet girl." She waved her bejeweled hand again. Her empty martini glass was whisked away and replaced with a fresh drink. She slipped the server another folded bill.

I had to admire her commitment to greasing the

wheels.

"Would you like a drink, Beth?" Gertrude asked, sloshing her martini.

"No, thank you. Not much of a drinker," I lied even as I thought of ways to punish my "uncle" for making me miss out on the creamy white pina coladas making the rounds. Apparently, Rob's "niece" didn't drink alcohol. Lucky for him, I didn't like to drink when I was working a job. Otherwise, my imaginary punishment would have been a lot bloodier.

I'm not a violent person. Don't like it at all, really. But there's only so much vacation-shattering a woman can take before she does start to let her imagination wander into new territory.

"Rob tells me your charity needs investors," Gertrude said before taking a long sip on her martini.

"We're looking for some now, yes," I said. And left it at that. No push. No ask.

"He's mentioned I might be interested?"

"Oh. I hadn't realized, no. I was under the impression you wanted to make a donation? Anything you might want to donate would be welcomed, really. We have a website, that might be easier. When we're in dock, of course." Internet access out at sea cost a fortune because you could only manage it through the cruise ship. Talk about a scam.

"Anyone can make donations," Gertrude said.

"And every one of the donations are greatly

appreciated." My most earnest voice. Rob gave me side-eye, but I ignored it. I knew my role here.

Gertrude's expression softened into an indulgent smile. "Ah, the idealism of youth. So sweet. I miss being that idealistic."

"Well, I don't know if it's idealism exactly…" I blushed and looked away. Yes, I can blush. On command even. I am very good at what I do. "I just like to help."

"Of course you do," Geraldine said. She glanced at Rob. "I wasn't convinced I'd do this before, but… I'd very much like to invest in your charity's new direction, Beth. It sounds splendid. And I like to put my considerable money to good use."

"That's so very kind of you." I let the flustered, slightly breathless quality rise in my voice. "I… I don't know what to say. Are you certain? I mean… Oh, are you sure?"

She chuckled. "I've done my research. I'd like to invest. A substantial amount of money. The lawyers can work out the details of course."

"Of course."

"But to prove my sincerity, I will transfer a substantial amount to your charity today. Would you like that?"

"Oh, really, that's too quick. Don't you want to examine contracts and everything first. It can wait. I know we might lose the—" I broke off and said, "No, that's not important. It's important to me that you are comfortable with your investment before you hand over money. We should do contracts first."

Nothing like trying to get someone to *not* give you money when they're trying to give you money.

We went on like this for a solid ten minutes before Rob gave me a subtle knee nudge. I could have pushed it out another three full minutes before it got ridiculous and obvious. I knew what I was doing. But this was his con, so I stopped arguing and let her talk me into taking some immediate capital to pay for the "facility the charity was in danger of losing if we didn't get money to the leasing agent by tomorrow."

Yes, Rob had told Gertrude "my secret" and put a tight deadline on the need for investment. Pretty clever. Getting to contracts and lawyers was always a lot trickier to swing. This gave Gertrude a reason to jump that part of the process and just drop us a small fortune.

It was also risky.

I gave Uncle Rob side-eye. "I wish you hadn't told her about that." I faced Gertrude again. "We can find another location. Eventually. It might take us longer to get the new aquatic center open, but we'll make it work. I don't like rushing people. Especially when it comes to money."

"My dear, I'm an excellent judge of character. You get to be my age, you learn a few things. Especially when you're rich as Midas. Lot of people want my money. I only give it when I'm content to."

"Still…"

"If you keep arguing with me, I'm going to get grumpy. Now stop. The money's yours. Today. I just need the information for wiring the funds."

"From here? How?" Which was actually a good question. I was sure Rob had it all figured out. Maybe Gertrude had sprung for the patchy open ocean wi-fi. But I was curious if Gertrude was prepared for giving away all this money from a cruise ship, or if she'd made the decision just now.

She waved a bejeweled hand again, the sunlight sparkling off some of the diamonds. A passing woman glanced longingly at Gertrude's hand and the man walking with her started to fidget and hurry the woman on. Either he was about to drop a lot of money on buying his girl jewelry at the boutiques downstairs, or that young woman was about to pull off a theft of her own.

Not that I considered what I did theft. Not in a technical sense of the word. I was a con artist. What I committed was fraud—if it ever got to court.

Gertrude said, "I have people for that. Rich as Midas remember. I just need the account number and access to a phone."

The speed and efficiency with which Gertrude managed to get said small fortune transferred to the account number Rob gave her—one opened under the name of the bogus charity organization he'd set up— was truly awe-inspiring. I kind of hoped that one day I'd be both that rich and that efficient. Then I'd sit around the pool on a cruise ship sipping pina coladas and holding court like a queen.

4

The only problem with pulling a scam like that so early in the trip was that I then had to ensure every time I bumped into Gertrude I was still Beth the niece. Since we'd used the name I was using on the cruise anyway, at least I'd answer if she called me. But it was still going to put a crimp in my holiday. The ten percent of my take softened the blow.

Or I thought it would soften the blow. If I'd received my ten percent.

We were well out at sea and I was coming back to my room from yet another spa session, ready for a proper nap, when Rob waylaid me.

"Come with me," he growled.

I didn't have time to resist or respond. I felt the nudge of his gun at my back. "What the hell?" I murmured.

"What did you do with it?"

"With what?"

"The money, bitch. What did you do with it? How did you get it all transferred?"

"The… What?" I blame the superb massage I'd just had for being so slow on the uptake.

"The money in my account is gone. All of it."

Shit. I blinked a few times. "Not me. I am content with my ten percent."

But now I was wondering if that money had made my account. I have one for these sorts of transactions, and I always move the money from that account to untraceable accounts immediately after I receive funds. But there'd been delays in all the money movement, so I hadn't had time to shift my take yet.

"You're a liar. But you aren't going to double cross me and get away with it. Come on." He jerked my arm and put us both in motion.

I tripped along beside him as we went downstairs, and along a corridor on the same side of the boat. I had a horrible feeling I knew where we were going. Stalling and conning another con was not an easy thing to do, especially when he thinks he's been cheated.

Still, I tried. "Going to get my suitcase finally? Great. I've missed my own clothes." I searched that suitcase he'd planted on me and sure enough, there were hidden jewels ferreted away in the lining—

something that wouldn't have gotten through the security scanners, but Rob had had help with that. Anyway, I was tempted to keep the jewels, but as I mentioned, I'm not a thief. I was also pretty sure the jewels were hot, and I had more than enough heat in the tropical climate as it was, thank you very much.

So I'd tucked the suitcase to one side of my room and Rob had promised to exchange cases just as soon as all the financials cleared.

"I want my money back," he growled. "You can kiss your freedom goodbye if I don't get it."

"Don't have it. Didn't take it. Don't know what you're talking about."

The problem with being a professional liar, though, is that the people who know don't believe you even when you're telling the truth.

He pushed me into his room after unlocking the door, and I stumbled over the threshold. Only to see Gertrude trussed up on the bed, her hands taped together in front of her.

"What the hell have you done?" I swung to face Rob. Now that the door behind him was closed, he had the gun out in plain sight, swiveling the point of it between me and Gertrude.

"I have spent years on this and I will not lose out on my windfall now. You're going to transfer that money back to me, *Beth*, or so help me god, I will shoot the old lady."

"Wait, what?" I moved a little so I was standing in front of Gertrude. Conning her was one thing. Murder something else altogether. I did not go in for murder. "That's crazy. You have to think about this. There's no way your guy in security will be able to get you out of a murder."

"He will if everyone thinks you're the killer. What with all that stolen loot in your suitcase."

I scowled. "First of all...stolen loot? Really? Couldn't have just said jewelry like an ordinary person? Second, I don't even know how to use a gun." Lie. "Why and how would I shoot Gertrude? In your room?"

"Oh, don't worry. I have that part all worked out."

That made me think he'd had it "worked out" from the beginning. But maybe not something he intended to pull the trigger on—so to speak—this soon.

And here he was accusing me of double crossing all my partners. Bastard. I, at least, had the decency to not kill anyone or frame them for murder when I double crossed them.

"I don't know where your money is. I haven't even checked my own account yet today." I held my hands up and back closer to Gertrude.

She was sitting on the bed, next to, of all things, my open suitcase. Everything in it had been tossed around, making a mess of the piles of clothes and shoes. The fact that Rob had my suitcase open and was going through my stuff was pretty skeevy. I'd have to wash every article of clothing before I could stomach wearing it. Probably should just buy new underwear, too.

"Why the hell were you going through my case, by the way?" I asked, gesturing at it with one hand while I motioned Gertrude to raise her hands to my back. I'd had my nails done in the spa yesterday evening, and had gotten a particularly nice set of tips. Sharp. Solid. Impossible to break, the lady had told me.

I flicked a finger at her and poked it at the tape, then held that finger still while she whimpered like she was terrified and hid behind me.

"I couldn't afford to leave anything ignored, could I?" Rob said.

"You think I keep account numbers and stuff like that in a notebook in my suitcase? How dumb to you think I am?"

"I don't. And now you're going to prove it by giving me my money back. Now. Or I will shoot her."

Gertrude hid farther behind me, make some mumbling noises around the gag he had in her mouth.

"You can't just go shooting old ladies, Rob," I said, "especially ones rich as Midas, and expect to get away with it. Even framing me isn't going to work." I felt the tape give. I needed to go back after this and tip that manicurist an extra twenty for the rock-solid tips.

"Stop stalling." He held out a cellphone—he must have paid for the extra wi-fi, too. Everyone was a money bags, just dropping outrageous fees for wi-fi. "Call whatever bank you've moved my money to, get them to move it back. All of it this time."

"You stealing my ten percent now, too? What a bastard." I shifted a little from one foot to the other.

"I don't share with people who double cross me."

"Rich. Since you intended on double crossing me."

He opened his mouth to say something, and the next moment he was struggling with a swan-shaped towel in his face.

The distraction lasted a full three seconds, not long at all. But long enough.

I grabbed the plastic-covered dildo baton from my bag and brought it down across his wrist with a crack. The gun hit the deck. Rob's wrist looked…not good.

He screamed and lunged at me. I brought the baton around and wacked him in the side of the head. Another crack. Then Rob hit the deck.

Hopefully I hadn't killed him. I'd like to see him in cuffs. I would enjoy that scene.

Gertrude stood up beside me.

"Thanks for the towel distraction," I said.

"That's some mighty dick you have there."

I hefted the baton disguised as a dildo. "It's got good weight."

"Have one myself in my luggage. They're handy, aren't they?"

We both looked at the unconscious conman on the ground at our feet.

"Handy alright," I said. I faced her. "You moved the money back out after you transferred it?"

"I never trusted him. Look at his face? He might as well have a sign that says, 'I'm a conman.' And bringing in disabled children." She tsked.

"I'm thinking you might be more familiar with the whole con game than you let on."

Gertrude smiled. "In my youth." She let out a sigh. "At any rate, your performance was exemplary. He blackmailed you to get you to help?"

"Yup."

"That's why I always worked alone."

"Me too! Partners are a pain in the ass."

"Oh, my dear, you have no idea." She went to the room phone beside the wide bed.

"Who are you calling?"

"*My* man on the security team. She's the head of the detail on this ship and has no time for people like Rob York. She'll ensure everything is set to rights. And she'll be very interested to hear one of her own team has been working with this criminal."

"What about me?" I asked. I didn't want to go to jail. But I figured, I could get off with self-defense, maybe manage some sort of plea for parole since I'd saved someone's life with my dildo baton. I'd work it out. So long as Gertrude was fine and Rob was not, I was going to call this situation a win.

I really had to give up my delusions of Love Boat cruises, though.

"Don't worry," Gertrude said with a wink. "Once this old lady has finished the telling, they'll be giving you free drinks and vouchers for future cruises and probably a medal. Trust me."

"I want to be you when I grow up."

She preened a little before launching into a truly impressive performance for the security person she'd reached.

I glanced down at Rob.

I don't trust other cons. We're not a trustworthy group. But between the two of them…

Yeah, I'll take the cunning old lady any day.

A Vacation to Die For

1

Casey Logan laid in bed, staring up at the dark thatched wood roof of the little open-sided bungalow, breathing in the salty ocean air, the night thickly humid, a cool breeze through the open walls keeping things cool and fresh, the moonless night ensuring deep shadows. She listened to the waves swishing gently underneath her, the sound of the waving palm tree fronds back up on the beach…

And the click of a cocked gun.

A gun. All the way out here. When she was supposed be on vacation with not a soul around to disturb her peace and quiet.

Someone was about to get hurt.

The little island off the coast of Bali only had about two dozen people on it. Three couples and one other single traveler, all occupying individual hunts at the ends of wooden docks out over the shallow blue ocean. Each hut spaced far enough apart to maximize privacy. The rest of the people on the island were resort staff, who lived here permanently, providing meals and fresh linens and emergency help if such were required by the vacationing tourists.

White sandy beaches, palm trees surrounded by leafy ferns, birds and fish and the occasional cockroach. No rats, though. She'd been delighted by the lack of rats. The resort was only accessible by boat, was only about two miles around, and was surrounded by the bluest, clearest ocean she'd ever seen in her life. Since she was from New York, that wasn't hard to accomplish. The Hudson was as opposite to clearest and bluest as water could get.

Her intent on this vacation, in this particular bungalow, with the ocean sweeping beneath her over shallow sand and reef, had been to nap, eat, and read every single paperback novel she'd stuffed into her luggage. She only needed minimal clothing in the tropical climate, which left more room for books. No technology. No phones. No jobs.

And she was supposed to have a full three weeks of just this.

The click of that gun meant her vacation was over.

She sighed. Rolled in the direction opposite the gun, dropped from the bed, hitting the wooden plank floor with a thunk, and slid underneath the bed frame, another beautiful collection of wood and thatch that had made for extremely cozy sleeping.

Curses to her left. "Where'd she go?"

She shook her head. Not even professionals. Thugs. She should have guessed when they made enough noise to warn her. Sending idiot thugs to interrupt her vacation. That was just insulting.

Someone was going to pay for that.

She waited until they were farther into the interior of the open-walled bedroom. Then she pushed the bed up with feet and hands, tossing it in the intruders' general direction.

By the time they'd finished cursing and had shoved the heavier-than-it-looked piece of furniture out of their way, she'd grabbed her waterproof go-bag and dove into the ocean.

A bullet whizzed wildly overhead, digging into the water a few feet from her. But the moonless night gave her good cover. They were shooting blind.

Amateurs.

Casey stayed underwater, swimming beneath the bungalow in the opposite direction from where she'd hit the water. She surfaced when she was on the far side of the hut, coming up silently and taking in enough air for another dive just as quietly.

There was a lot of cursing from the hut, a lot of knocking things around. Some of her paperbacks were tossed out the side of the building. She watched the pages flutter as the books splashed down into the waves.

They weren't just going to pay now. They were going to pay with pain. Lots and lots of pain.

The beam of a wildly swinging flashlight forced her to dive before the light caught her.

She slipped close to the beach before surfacing again, letting the waves roll her toward shore so she could minimize the strokes she had to take, making it harder to spot her in the shallow swells. The men had left her hut and were running along the long wooden dock back to the beach, the beams of their flashlights still flailing around as they ran.

Hadn't even thought to turn the lights off. She sighed.

Whoever had hired them was going to get her foot up their ass at her earliest convenience.

Really, if you were going to send people to kill her, at least do her the courtesy of sending professionals. This was an insult to her professional pride.

She waited in the waves, just off shore, watching the chaos. There were three of them all together. The two that had come out to the bungalow and one still on shore. The one on shore was yelling at the other two, not even bothering to keep his voice down. Given the nearest bungalow was around a bend in the island, she supposed she could understand his mistake. But sound carried across the water.

Someone had heard those gunshots.

Unfortunately, that meant some poor sod was about to walk into the middle of all this and get themselves shot. She didn't trust the idiots not to just kill any witnesses. You couldn't trust amateurs not to panic.

And from all the noise they were making, they were panicking.

What a pain in her ass. All she'd wanted was three weeks of novel reading and naps. Was that too much to ask?

She swam gently to a section of beach where the beach was narrow and the trees came close to the water. Slipping out as a set rolled in, she let the pounding thud of the waves against the sand cover her movements. Though why she bothered... The thugs were making so much noise she wasn't sure they'd hear a troop of walruses marching out of the ocean.

She hit the cover of the trees without drawing any attention.

2

T he three amateur assassins charged up and down the beach, looking out at the water, their flashlights hunting vainly in the rolling waves.

Nowhere near where she'd come ashore.

Squatting behind a crop of pale rocks inside the swaying palm trees, she unrolled the top of her go-bag and pulled out a hair clip, wrapping her wet hair up into a bun so it would be out of the way. Then quickly changed from the soaking wet t-shirt and pajama shorts she'd worn to bed and into a wet suit that would give her some flexibility with what she did next. The moonless night was humid and warm, but she hadn't been dressed for a late night swim.

No gun because she was *on vacation*, but she belted on the diving knife in her pack. She considered the nine inch flashlight, but she was better off maintaining her night vision, so she left it.

She rolling down the top and quietly clipped it closed, then slid her arms through the straps, wearing the bag as a backpack so she could keep her hands free.

Then she started across the edge of the beach, keeping to the trees.

The dumb bastards were still watching the water. What'd they think, she was mermaiding around out there waiting for them to leave?

She snuck up behind them without effort—and wasn't that just annoying. Not one of them turned when she stepped out of the cover of trees to stand on the beach.

Hands on her hips, she hung her head and sighed. Amateurs.

She cleared her throat.

All three swung to face her, their flashlight beams whizzing wildly around the sparse tropical jungle at her back. She'd counted to twenty before one of the beams finally caught her.

"So slow," she muttered. "You realize I could have killed all three of you before you knew I was out of the water? What the hell?"

"Stay where you are," one of them, the one who'd remained on the beach, snapped. Then in what he probably thought was a calming tone said, "We're not here to hurt you."

She gave him a look. He had the decency to wince and glance away.

Waving his gun vaguely in her direction without looking at her, he said, "It's nothing personal, see."

"Oh I see, all right." She took in all three men in one sweeping glance. Mid-twenties, maybe pushing thirties, white, all three of them thick shouldered, one a little thick around the middle, the other two relatively trim, all wearing some variation on tank tops and board shorts, their Tevas wet and sandy now.

She flexed her bare toes in the soft, cool sand.

All three had guns pointed at her and little flashlight beams wavering over her. Did they realize the jumping beams were a tell? Probably not.

"Who sent you?" she asked.

"It's nothing personal, see," the one who seemed to be the leader said.

"Yeah, we're just doing a job," another one said. He was shorter and squatter than the leader, his brown hair lanky and in need of a trim.

"A job," the third said, punctuating his statement by jabbing his gun in the air.

"For who?" she asked again, trying to be patient.

Second Guy said, "And Anders said—"

"Shut up," the leader snapped.

She frowned at all three men. Anders, huh.

Anders was a dodgy businessman who had

delusions of being a criminal king pin. He'd attempted, on more than one occasion, to make good at those delusions by hiring her. She'd turned him down. She was particular about who she worked with.

Since he was the sensitive type, with an ego the size of Queens, he hadn't been pleased with her refusing his jobs. He might well want to kill her. But he should have known better than to send amateurs after her.

"What did you do to piss him off?" she asked.

"What'd you mean?" Second Guy, trying to look tough.

"Shut up," Leader hissed. "We aren't here to talk about that," he said to her.

"So you did piss him off," she said.

"No. That's… I didn't say that."

"You did steal his truck," Third Guy said.

"Did not," Leader snarled.

"It was his Porsche," Second Guy said.

"Damn straight," Leader said. "Not getting jammed up for stealing a fucking truck."

"You stole Anders' Porsche?" she asked.

Leader glared at the other two. Second Guy shrugged a little. Third Guy shuffled his feet in the sand.

"You know he loves that stupid car, right?" she asked.

"How was I supposed to know?" Leader waved

his own gun around to emphasize his point. "Gorgeous Porsche just sitting there. Keys in the ignition. How was I supposed to know who it belonged to? He didn't leave a fucking sign, did he?"

"The license plate has his name on it."

"Wasn't looking at the plate, was I?"

"Do next time. Could save your life."

"I don't take advice from cheating ex-mistress thieves," Leader snarled.

She blinked at him. "Say that again."

"You heard me, bitch."

"He told you…" She cleared her throat. "He told you I was an ex-mistress?"

"And that you stole a million from him. He wants his money back."

"And he don't care how we get it," Second Guy said.

Third Guy lifted his lip in a smirk. His flashlight beam still wavered.

"Wow." She considered the sand for a long moment. "Yeah. You guys really pissed him off, stealing the Porsche. Sent you halfway around the world to be killed."

"What the fuck you talking about?" Second Guy said. "We're the ones with guns."

She swung her pack off her back, low and up, sending soft white sand flying into their faces. The breeze was at their backs, which made the sand thing less effective than it might have been if the wind was blowing off the low hills behind her. But these guys weren't the professionals she was used to dealing with.

They waved at the sand, cursing, coughing, their guns swinging wildly. One shot randomly in her general direction, hitting a palm tree.

She dove, rolled, and came up next to the Third Guy. She gave him a split second to blink at her before she slammed her go-bag—with the heavy flashlight inside—down onto his arm. He dropped his gun with a scream. She stepped on the gun at the same time as slamming her fist up under his chin.

She didn't wait to see him hit the ground, but did use his falling body as cover. Second Guy ducked and aimed his gun at her, but was obviously reluctant to shoot his comrade.

That redeemed him to her. A little. A very little.

She pushed Third Guy so he fell into Second Guy, sending Second Guy's arms flailing as he tried to catch Third Guy without dropping his gun. She spun past him, taking his gun and slamming the butt down on the back of his head before he had a chance to curse.

Second Guy and Third Guy both hit the sand with a thud as she swung to face Leader. He was pointing his gun at her, his gaze jumping between her and his two unconscious companions.

"What the hell?" he muttered.

"Anders didn't send you to rough up an ex-mistress for stolen money," she said. "There's no money. No mistress."

"Who the hell are you then?"

"Just a woman trying to relax on vacation. Read a few books. Dip my toes into the waves."

He reflexively glanced down at her feet. She kicked sand in his face, brought Second Guy's gun down across his wrist, cracking bone, and caught his dropped gun before it hit the ground.

He screamed and swung wildly around with his good arm, but she'd already moved behind him. She brought both gun butts down on the back of his skull, hard. And watched him fall face first into the sand.

"The broken wrist…" she said to the unconscious man. "That was for letting your boys ruin my books."

<h1 style="text-align:center">3</h1>

Casey had all three men duck taped to a palm tree by the time they regained consciousness. There was a lot of cursing when they realized they couldn't move.

"Right," she said, squatting down so she was eye-level with Leader. "You're gonna want to have that wrist looked at after someone spots you and cuts you out. Hopefully, that won't be too long. Breakfast is delivered at nine. You shout enough, someone'll probably hear. Since Anders sent you to get killed, I'm going to suggest you stay as far away from him as possible from now on. Find a nice safe town on the far side of the planet from him, and only boost the cars of normal people. No more stealing wealthy-wannabe-crime bosses' Porsches. 'Kay."

She patted Leader's cheek then stood.

While they'd been unconscious, she'd rinsed sand and saltwater off in the small freshwater shower in her bungalow. Then she'd repacked her single backpack with as many of the paperbacks as she could salvage, her scant few clothes, and returned her diving knife to the go-bag. She hadn't even bothered to use it on the men. She hated getting stupid people's blood on her good weapons.

She threw the backpack across her shoulders, carrying the go-bag by the top clip, and turned away from the men.

"Hey, hey! You can't just leave us here," Leader shouted at her back. "I got a broken wrist. There's no one around! You can't just leave."

She ignored his shouts as she dug her toes one last time in the brown sugar textured sand, breathing in the salt flavored air, disappointed her vacation had been cut short. More than disappointed.

She was pissed.

By the time the sun crested the horizon, painting the sky pink and orange, she was on a stolen speedboat, heading toward the mainland. And a flight to London.

She had a wannabe-crime-boss to see.

AT THE AIRPORT, USING A BURNER CELLPHONE SHE'D picked up from an acquaintance in Denpasar, she rang her associate, Nicky.

"Thought you were on holiday," Nicky said without preamble. "No phones, no technology. What happen, you get bored?"

"Anders sent some fellas to disrupt my peace and quiet."

She scanned the airport, sitting with her back to a wall. No one sat near her on the row of plastic seats, and she discouraged company with a pointed stare. The cacophony of shouting, talking tourists stomping past on the polished marble floors drown out the sounds of her conversation. Only one young Australian man gave her a second look, moved close enough to say hi, then hurriedly left after meeting her eyes.

"Anders tried to kill you?" Nicky said, nonplused. "Is he suicidal?"

"He sent three asshole amateurs."

"Amateurs? He sent amateurs? After you?"

"Sent them so I'd kill them."

"Without…booking you first? Without paying you?"

"Yup."

"While you were on *vacation*?"

"Hmm Umm."

"Well, that's insulting."

"That's what I said."

"Why'd he want them dead?"

"They boosted his Porsche."

"Shit. He loves that mid-life-crisis-I've-got-a-small-dick car."

"He surely does." She considered a busy restaurant across the corridor from where she sat. Steam rose from hotplates, and the smell of rice and spices made her stomach growl.

"Still," Nicky said, and sniffed. "Rude."

"Right?"

"And unprofessional."

"He told them I was an ex-mistress."

"Ew."

"As if."

The airport loudspeaker squawked on and a polished female voice announced in five different languages that her flight was boarding. Standing and sweeping up her backpack, she headed toward her gate, giving one last longing glance at the restaurant. Airplane food would have to do. Some end to her vacation.

"I'll be in London by tomorrow morning," she said. "Get me a meeting with Anders."

"Office or home?"

"That gawd awful townhouse he's been working on for forever. That'll do."

"You just want to see the library."

"Nicky, they dumped some of my paperbacks into the ocean. Before I'd got the chance to read them."

"Shit." There was a moment's silence for the loss. "Right. Home, it is, then. Want to meet Bruno before you go in?"

"Won't need to."

4

The massive white stone townhouse in the heart of Kensington was a point of pride for Anders. Just like his Porsche, the mansion was his "baby," and he'd spent years renovating it, ensuring it was just so. Hardwood, inlaid floors throughout. Marble accents. Sweeping staircases with intricately, hand-carved wooden banisters. Light wood wainscoting under pale wallpaper. Art to rival a museum's hanging on those wall.

Not that she recognized any of it. She wasn't a thief so she hadn't bothered to study that sort of thing. But she knew Anders, so she assumed everything hanging, sitting on the tiny wooden tables, and tucked into the decorative insets in the walls was all valuable and showed the world what a big shot lived there. Anders would accept nothing less.

Such a fucking poser.

After she'd been searched for weapons, a liveried butler—more posing—led her into a giant library. And here, finally, she was impressed.

Massive windows looking out onto the gray London street beyond. A giant wooden desk sat in front of the windows. Thick Turkish rugs over the inlaid floors. And wall-to-wall, floor-to-ceiling, light wood, fully packed bookshelves. Leather bound books mostly, at least at eye-level. But one of those tall ladders that slid along the cases gave access to the higher shelves, and up there she spotted regular paperbacks and hardcovers. That's where she'd spend most of her time. Up on the ladder pulling down novels to read.

The place smelled of leather, ink and paper, lemon-scented furniture polish, and just a hint of tea. The tea might be her imagination, though, since she was in England and everyone here was obsessed with the stuff.

Two wing-backed, green leather chairs sat in front of a giant marble and stone fireplace to the left. And that's where Anders waited for her. The butler left her at the door. She took a seat next to Anders. He didn't stand. Given the setting, she sort of thought he might.

Anders—one name only because he was a poser wannabe crime boss—was a relatively unimpressive looking man. Average height, average weight, fit enough but not thick, dark hair trimmed neat and short, blue eyes behind tiny round-rimmed glasses that were just for show, a kind of pinched mouth that reminded her of the disapproving head mistress at the girls school she'd attended for exactly two months before being kicked out.

He wore a garishly neon green track suit that was probably from a brand that cost as much as an average Londoner's monthly rent, but it looked like ordinary nylon running pants and zip-up hoodie to her. He wore a gold Rolex. And she suspected his runners were custom made by one of the big tennis shoe companies. But you'd have had to know these fashion-related things to look at him and say, "Wealth!"

Mostly, he looked like someone trying to look like a hoodlum trying to look like a big man. But he ended up just looking like a muddled mess. Fake glasses with a track suit and a Rolex… The combination made her eyes hurt.

"Sherry," he offered, gesturing to a crystal decanter and cut-crystal glasses sitting on a little wooden table between them. He had a relatively ordinary voice, too. Posh, flat London accent he'd worked years to train, but otherwise, nothing particularly special in his voice. Not too deep, not too high. Just…ordinary.

Lot of ordinary for a wannabe criminal king pin.

"No," she said. "Alcohol gives me headaches."

"Shame. How do you relax?"

She gestured at the books. "Read. You?"

"Drive very fast in my Porsche."

"I told them they'd really pissed you off trying to steal that thing."

"They should have checked the car's plates."

She smacked the arm of the chair, then pointed at him. "That's what I told them. Thugs." She shook her head mournfully. "At any rate, sending them to me to be killed without paying me first was very cheeky of you."

"Did you kill them?"

"Yes," she lied straight-faced.

"Then I'll pay you."

That wasn't how her business worked. But she'd deal with that in a minute. "What were they worth to you?"

"Ten each?"

She snorted. "Your Porsche is worth a couple mil. Custom made and all that. You're insulting me yet again."

He flattened his mouth. "Fine. A hundred each."

She raised her brows.

"They were knackers. You didn't have to do much. Can't imagine they even got close enough to be a threat. They weren't worth more than a hundred each."

She continued to stare at him.

He turned away first. "Fine. Five hundred."

"Each."

His mouth worked, but he said, "Each."

"Pounds. Not dollars."

"Pounds. Five hundred thousand pounds each. Fair?"

She glanced at the fireplace. "That thing is massive. Aren't you afraid it'll catch the house on fire?"

"Hasn't yet."

"Yet being a very significant word here. You ever actually have fires in it, or is it just for show?"

"In London? Mostly just for show nowadays. Gets cold enough. But there are all kinds of air quality laws now."

"Fair enough. This city used to be gross. Couldn't be here more than twenty-four hours and I'd be cleaning black shit out of nose. Lot better now. Definitely."

"Is that all? Are we done here? I have other business."

"Now, here I've flown halfway around the world to see you. Cut my vacation short, just for this meeting. And that's all the time I get?"

"You're getting paid. Isn't that all that matters with your kind."

"My kind? That sounds like an insult Anders. That's rich. Pot kettle kind of comment."

"Your handler made the appointment last minute, or I would have booked more time for you."

"Sure." She stood. Waited for him to stand. When he didn't, she shook her head. No manners. Not even offering a handshake.

She stared down at the side of his face until he turned to look at her.

"What?" he demanded.

"You ruined my vacation, you know."

"I'm sure you can take another one."

"They dumped some of my books into the sea, Anders. My books." She glanced around the giant library.

"Books are replaceable."

"So's a car."

"Not this car."

"You would have paid less to just get another car."

"Even a million and a half wouldn't have replaced the car."

"Still. Lot less trouble. Lot less blood."

"What blood?"

She smashed the crystal cut decanter into his face. There was a very satisfying crunch. Blood poured out of his nose.

She shoved him back into the chair, pinning him in place with a knee to his groin, and an arm across his throat, and said near his ear, "Never send anyone at me like that again. I don't kill without payment."

"You think I'm gonna fucking pay you now? You just broke my fucking nose."

He opened his mouth to shout, but she stuck the heel of her hand against his already broken bone, pressing hard enough to make him whimper.

"Shhhh," she murmured. "I'm not done talking yet. I told you before I won't kill for you. Then you went and ruined my vacation. And your goons—who aren't dead, by the way, because I don't kill without payment—trashed some of my books. My books, Anders." She leaned in very close. "So now you're going to get that money into my account, without argument. Because if you don't, next time I won't bother with an appointment."

He tried to snarl, but with blood gushing down his face and over the horrid green track suit hoodie, the expression fell flat.

"One more thing," she said against his ear, while pressing her hand tight against his nose and grinding her knee down hard. "You'll find your Porsche parked at the bottom of the Thames."

She shoved away from him and shouted, "Help! Someone. Help!"

The butler pushed inside immediately—confirming he was more than just a liveried butler.

She pointed at Anders' nose and softened her voice, affecting shock and worry. "He needs help. He stood to shake my hand, slipped and smashed his face against the decanter. I think his nose is broken. I tried to stop the bleeding, but…" She made a helpless little gesture with her hands, fluttering them in distress. "Get someone. Quick."

The butler shouted down the hall, vanishing for a moment as he rallied the troops.

She met Anders' gaze and murmured, "I'll expect the money by five. If it's not there…"

"Why not just kill me now?" he muttered, looking at the blood on his hands.

"I don't kill unless I'm paid," she reminded him. Again. "Though, I could be pushed into making an exception. I don't recommend you push me. Consider the fee and the damage to the Porsche break even for my vacation. And my books." She smiled and said cheerily, "Enjoy the rest of your day."

Then she sauntered out of the magnificent library as a herd of Anders people rushed in to see to his bleeding face.

The money hit her account by four thirty.

She went right to the bookstore.

Darwin's Atoll

1

Marta listened to the ocean shoosh against the hull of the yacht, the distant sounds of sea birds squawking, breathed in the scents of salt air and machine oil…

And reconsidered all her life choices.

"You just had to steal a smuggler's yacht," she whispered to her soon-to-be strangled companion. "Couldn't steal an ordinary person's yacht. No. You had to steal a smuggler's yacht."

"I didn't do it on purpose," Jake muttered.

On purpose or not, they were now hiding behind machinery she couldn't identify in the yacht's engine room, tucked against the clean white hull, with no way to get off this boat without being killed.

So yeah, she was going to strangle him.

"There were other ways of getting out to the

atoll," she continued as if he hadn't spoken. "We could have actually paid one of the fishing boat captains."

"And risk someone realizing what we're doing, or worse seeing the treasure? No."

"If we even find it," she said.

The Lost Treasure of the HMS Beagle wasn't exactly a popular target for most treasure hunters because most of them thought it didn't exist. A ridiculous joke, most said. Nothing but fossil specimens, others claimed.

But if it did exist, if it was what she and Jake thought it was, it'd be the find of the century. Worth… Well, she couldn't calculate. But a lot. Enough to make their investment in this trip worthwhile.

Jake was probably right. Last thing they needed was someone else realizing what was, possibly, buried out at the atoll. They'd been double crossed once already, when the boat they'd originally rented sank before they'd left the pier. Risking someone getting wind of *why* they needed to get to the atoll so desperately would be bad.

Still. That didn't make her any happier about their current predicament.

The minute she'd opened the storage locker on the lower deck and discovered the racks of guns and drugs, she'd known they were in trouble. She'd barely had time to show Jake the mess they were in before the sounds of a rapidly approaching speedboat sent them scrambling for cover.

"How the hell are we going to get out of this?" she hissed.

"First. Shut up. They're going to hear you. Second. I'm working on it…"

"Last time you worked on something we ended up on a smuggler's boat."

They'd ducked behind cover and watched just long enough to see who boarded the yacht, just long enough to make absolutely certain they were fucked. And they were. The two upper decks were now filled with people in dark sunglasses, toting intimidatingly large guns, and saying things like, "The goods are fine. The thieves didn't get them."

Thieves! As if.

She and Jake had ducked into the yacht's engine room before they were spotted, tucked back behind the machinery, hoping the guys with guns walking around the sixty foot yacht didn't discover them. Which seemed very unlikely, given the guys with the guns were highly motivated to find the fools who'd stolen the yacht. And the yacht wasn't *that* big. For a yacht.

With luck, the guys with guns would think Marta and Jake had ditched the yacht in the lifeboat they'd jettisoned.

She'd argued they should get *on* the lifeboat as a

means of escape. Jake had argued the guys with the guns would spot them too easily, and they needed the lifeboat as a decoy. She'd argued that without it, they had no way to get off the ship.

He'd jettisoned the lifeboat anyway, claiming he had a plan.

He didn't have a plan. He had a hiding spot. Which was not the same as an escape plan.

The yacht engines roared to life around them, loud enough to drown out the sounds of the waves and any hope they had of hearing someone approach.

Helpful.

The boat lurched. She braced against the hull as Jake fell into her, his weight pressing her harder into the side of the boat.

They both stayed that way as the engine noise settled, and they heard shouts from above.

"I think they've found the lifeboat," he murmured in her ear.

A rapid round of gunfire. Something exploded.

Marta ducked instinctively. Then closed her eyes and sighed.

"Lifeboat?" she whispered in Jake's ear.

"Lifeboat." He dropped his forehead to the hull next to her head.

Under different circumstances, Marta might have comforted Jake, reminded him this wasn't his fault.

Except it was all his fault and she was going to strangle him when—*if*—they got out of this.

"Did you know that would happen?" she asked.

"That they'd blow up the lifeboat? Yeah. Sure. Why do you think I didn't want us on it?"

She gave him a look. He refused to meet her gaze.

"Now what?"

"Plan A just got blown up," he said. "Still working on a plan B."

"We can't swim all the way to the atoll." They were still a mile from the little island that was all that remained of a buried volcano. And far enough from the Tahiti mainland, they'd be eaten by sharks well before they ever saw land.

"Might have to try," he muttered.

They'd come prepared to dive, but their diving gear was up on the swim platform on the middle deck—or maybe dropped overboard into the ocean by now. She'd heard a splash earlier. Hard to tell what had gone in. Dive gear. One of the smugglers. Dead body.

Probably where the smugglers would dump Marta and Jake's dead bodies.

She gave herself a mental shake and tried to pull it together. They wouldn't have dive gear, so even if they reached the water, they couldn't hide below the surface. And swimming above the surface made them easy targets for the smugglers.

And even if the smugglers somehow missed them

in the wide open ocean, the sharks most assuredly would not.

The boat lurched to one side, the turn pushing them against the hull again, before jumping forward. With the engines running, she couldn't hear what was going on outside anymore. And that felt dangerous.

"Should we make a run for it? While we're moving?"

Jake shook his head. "Too many of them. They'd see us before we hit the water."

There were a lot of nooks and crannies and hiding places on a sixty-foot yacht—thus the guns and drugs —but there'd also been at least a dozen guys with guns who'd boarded the ship. Enough to space out and keep watch.

"With luck, they think they've blown us up in the lifeboat," Jake said.

Luck.

That was a funny word to use for what they'd been having.

2

Minutes ticked by, but no one came into the engine room. The yacht cut over the waves at a smooth clip Marta could feel through the hull, but without windows, she had no idea if they were headed back to Tahiti or somewhere else.

"We'll wait until the boat stops," Jake said. "Once they're distracted with…whatever they're going to do when they get where they're going, we can sneak off. They'll never be the wiser."

"That's your plan?"

"You have a better one?"

"No."

"Then that's my plan."

She pulled in a deep breath and let it out very slowly so she wouldn't cuss.

After a few more minutes, she pushed him away

from her and settled down on the deck, wedging herself between clean, sparkling engine parts. If they had to wait, she'd wait in comfort. Or relative comfort. The roughened, non-slip surfacing on the floor poked her hands and snagged at her running shorts. But it was better than being shot.

And it wasn't like there was anywhere to run if the smugglers came looking for them here.

After a minute, Jake sat down next to her, leaning back against the hull. "Sorry about this."

She waved away his apology. "If we survive, buy me a beer and we'll call it even."

He nodded.

"Sorry I lured you into another adventure," she said after a moment.

He waved away her apology with the same gesture she'd used. "We find the Beagle treasure, we'll call it even."

She huffed out a silent chuckle.

Silence. She strained to hear around the noise of the engines, but unlike above decks, where the engine room's insulation kept all the noise dampened, the engine room itself was a cacophony. No hope of hearing anything.

She tapped her foot against the floor in a rapid staccato. This felt like playing hide and seek. Just sitting here. Waiting to be found.

She hated hide and seek.

"My brother asked your sister out," Jake said, breaking into her spiraling thoughts.

"What?" She faced him. "What is your fool little brother doing hitting my baby sister?"

"I warned him it was a bad idea," Jake said, staring ahead, not looking at her.

She leaned back against the wall. "If he hurts her, I'm gonna kill him."

"Told him that."

She considered the situation. Then shrugged. "She'll probably shoot him before I can get to him."

"Told him that, too."

They both nodded, staring straight ahead. It didn't matter that their siblings were fully grown adults and federal agents with the FBI. They were both younger siblings and that meant they were a pain in the ass for their older siblings.

Although, Marta was pretty sure her sister would claim it was the other way around.

She blinked at the white casing and black pipes across from her as something truly horrible occurred to her.

She faced Jake again. "What if works out between them?"

He finally turned to face her, his green eyes wide. "Fuck me."

Before he could say more, the engine noise changed and the boat slowed.

Without a word, they both rose to their feet, staying crouched behind the engine room machinery. Marta strained to hear anything at all from outside the closed room.

"Should we make a run for it?" she murmured.

He remained silent, his expression distant.

The engines quieted, then fell silent. Marta shook her head a little, hoping to clear the ringing in her ears faster so she could hear what was happening above decks.

They could still be out in the middle of the ocean somewhere. Which meant running wasn't any more of an option now than it had been when the guys with guns had come aboard.

Then, from the front of the boat, she heard something very heavy hit the water.

"A body?" she murmured.

"The anchor," Jake said, frowning.

Noise from above. Men shouting at each other. The sound of another boat engine passing the side of the yacht. Stomping and shouts and noises she couldn't identify.

"Can you tell what's happening?"

"Not sure. But…" His frown deepened. "Sounds like they're unloading the guns and stuff."

"That good or bad for us?"

"Depends on where we are."

More shouts, more movement above deck.

When they heard movement and noise just outside the engine room's overhead hatch, she and Jake moved back farther against the hull, pressing into the cool fiberglass.

Marta held her breath, expecting the hatch to open at any moment. She'd swear someone stopped at it, could practically feel someone staring at it.

Then footsteps. And whoever had been there moved on.

The sound of the other boat engine roared to life. Then things got very quiet.

They waited in silence for long enough Marta started tapping her foot against the deck again. Her soft-soled deck shoes kept her from making too much nose, but still she made an effort to still the fidget.

When they hadn't heard anything for a full five minutes except the distant sound of the other boat engine stopping, Jake said, "Let's go."

She wanted to ask questions. Instead, she followed silently, her heart pounding hard in her chest, her pulse raising, her gut tight.

She liked an adventure as much as the next woman. But this was a little much. Even for her.

3

When they reached the middle deck without being caught, Marta almost whimpered in relief at the sight of the small island just off the port side of the yacht. The yacht was anchored in a rounded inlet within easy swimming distance of the white sandy beach and shady palms.

The salty tang in the hot air, and the anxiety sweat under her t-shirt beading along her spine, had her itching to dive into the crystal-clear blue waters. Anything to get off this yacht.

"I don't believe it," Jake murmured beside her.

They'd crawled and edged their way to a narrow section off the middle deck, aft, close to the swim platform. Their dive gear was gone, as she'd feared, and she sighed at the loss of such expensive equipment. But at least there was land nearby.

"What?" she asked, leaning close so they could keep their voices from carrying.

The ocean breeze was cool and fresh after being below deck, helping dry the sweat on her skin. But just beyond the shade where they hid, the sun was high and hot. Summer in the South Pacific.

"That's the atoll," Jake said against her ear.

"No way." She looked again. This time studying the layout of the island, the formation of the inlet. "You're sure?"

"Based on the satellite pictures? Yeah. I'm sure."

"Why are *they* here?"

She was certain the smugglers weren't here for the Beagle treasure. It was a joke among treasure hunters, the few who'd even heard of it. Gun runners surely wouldn't know about it.

The supposed lost treasure of the HMS Beagle wasn't even a very popular conspiracy theory. She hadn't heard about it. And she was a science historian who did like the occasional treasure hunt. If there'd been a secret treasure associated with Darwin, she thought for sure she'd have heard about it.

So when she'd stumbled across a passage in one of Charles Darwin's sister's diaries, written during the years he'd been aboard the Beagle, she hadn't given the information much thought.

Until she'd mentioned it to Jake.

Jake was the one who told her about the supposed Lost Beagle Treasure. How the idea of it was laughed at by even the most ardent treasure hunters. But the legend of a golden box holding a golden statue that Darwin found while he was stomping through the jungle in Brazil lingered, even if no one really believed it.

According to Jake, the legend said the box was cursed and caused the Beagle crew no end of trouble. So Captain FitzRoy insisted they get rid of it, despite its value, in a place no one would ever find it. And proceeded to wipe all records of the existence of the box from the crew's official documents and diaries. Apparently, the curse was bad enough to keep everyone quiet about the box. Even Darwin, who wrote every day in his diaries while at sea.

But this one entry in his sister Caroline's diary discussed something he'd said to her in a letter, a letter which was later destroyed. Darwin apparently mentions the Beagle had stopped just after leaving Tahiti to discard a "cursed and unholy mistake" at a small atoll, so the "native demons" would no longer follow their crew around.

Caroline described the "mistake" as a golden box and mentioned a few details about the atoll, its direction and distance from Tahiti, some of the flora and fauna, all relayed by Darwin. Beyond that, there was no other record or mention of such a finding anywhere.

Marta assumed Caroline had gotten some of the details wrong, that the "golden box" was figurative rather than literal. Hearing the story existed outside that one passage, even as a joke, had fired up both her and Jake's curiosity.

Unfortunately, that curiosity had gotten them into this mess.

"Do you see any of the smugglers?" she asked.

"Just the boat." He nodded to where a motorboat had run up onto the sand. No sign of the men.

"Our bad luck this atoll is used as a gun and drug drop?"

"Very bad luck," Jake said.

"If there was a treasure here, gun runners would probably have found it by now."

"Not necessarily."

Jake had done more research into the legend. Since most of it was second hand rumors from people who'd talked about it in drunken states, there wasn't a lot to go on. But enough to know that the Beagle crew had buried the box and covered it with a cross in an attempt to break the curse.

"The cross probably makes it look like a rudimentary grave," he whispered. "If they're the superstitious types, they wouldn't mess with it."

She had no idea if smugglers were superstitious or

not, but she was hoping they were. "Do we go ashore?"

That was safer than the yacht. But they'd be stuck out on this atoll with little hope of rescue once the smugglers left.

"Yes," Jake said. "But we need a few things first."

4

They surfaced as far from the beached motorboat as they could manage and hurried up the short run of white sand to the cover of palm trees and thick fern underbrush. Once inside the cool, shady jungle, Marta let out a long breath. She was an excellent swimmer, but her heart was pounding hard from fear.

Skimming a hand over her damp hair, and squeezing out some of the water in her ponytail, she said, "Do we wait until they leave, or start searching now?"

"No idea where they are. But I don't want to wait too long. We'll search. But carefully. Any noise, we take cover."

She nodded. They'd planned on this search taking several days. They were pretty sure the Beagle crew wouldn't have gone too deep into the atoll, since this was a spontaneous stop and they wouldn't have wanted to stay here very long. Beyond that, the atoll itself wasn't very big. Maybe three miles around, two miles wide at the thickest sections.

Between the two of them, scouting the empty jungle, they'd figured they'd need three days at the most to find the box's "grave."

That had been before the smugglers.

As the afternoon heat thickened the humid air under the palms, Marta and Jake quietly worked their way through the jungle, walking in the opposite direction of the motorboat.

Without having any idea where the smuggles were, Marta's skin prickled with nerves, anticipating hearing them at any moment. So much of her focus was on the surrounding trees, looking out for signs of other humans, she forgot to search for something that looked like a cross-marked grave.

So when she literally stumbled against the small stone and wood cross and fell into the ferns, it came as a shock.

Jake's expression was carefully neutral as he helped her back to her feet. She scowled, brushing off her hands and shorts. Then stopped mid-motion.

They both stared at the cross.

A pile of stones built up around two pieces of rough beach bark lashed together with a thick rope to form a rudimentary cross shape. The ground around the cross was remarkably clear of overgrowth. Moss grew on the wood and rope.

Marta squatted down in front of the cross and ran her fingers over the rough twine rope. Just at the intersection of the two pieces of wood, right above the rope, someone had carved a little symbol that looked like a lizard.

She ran a finger over the carving. Then looked up at Jake. "It's here," she mouthed, her eyes wide, breaking out into a grin despite their still precarious situation.

He grinned back, his cheeks red from the heat, sweat slicking down his dark brown hair.

The heat and sweat and humidity hardly mattered now. They'd found it!

Whatever it turned out to be, the fact that there *was* a cross marked spot here on this specific atoll was almost all the thrill Marta needed.

Jake would want the treasure, though.

They unhooked the waterproof backpacks they'd strapped on before leaving the yacht—bags they'd brought with them but that had been fortunately missed by the smugglers—and got to work digging.

Because they'd lost a lot of their gear, they had to dig with the little trowels they had inside their bags. Not easy. But manageable.

The sound of metal hitting something hard, made

them both pause. She stared at Jake for a heartbeat, before digging frantically around the spot she'd just made contact with something.

The wink of gold through the dark soil made her heartbeat race.

"I can't believe it," Jake murmured. "I was convinced we'd find an old chest full of fossils and nothing of real value."

"Really? Then why come all this way?"

"You wanted to." He shrugged, his gaze on the gold. "And I can't resist a mystery."

She glanced from him back to the gold edge visible through the dirt. She couldn't resist a mystery either.

And they'd just discovered one hell of a treasure.

DIGGING THE SMALL CHEST OUT OF THE LOOSE DIRT took some time and effort. Hauling the thing free of the earth took both of them. The box was a lot heavier than she'd been expecting, even if it contained the fabled golden statue that was the supposed source of all the trouble.

The outside of the box, the chest itself, was treasure enough. Encased almost entirely in gold, which likely had preserved the wood beneath, the box was roughly two feet by one foot. The gold was decorated with images of animals and markings that reminded her vaguely of the sort of pictographic writing used by the…Inca, maybe? Not her specialty, but they had time to figure it out.

There was a clip on the box, holding the lid closed, but no apparent locks or seals.

"Should we open it?" she asked.

Jake looked around. "It's too big to sneak easily around with. I'd rather open it in a more secured place, but…"

"But what if its empty?"

He shrugged. "Even if its empty, the box itself is worth a small fortune."

"What if there's something living in here?" she said. Not that she figured there was much on the island that could have gotten into the chest without leaving some evidence of its existence on the outside. Still. She'd had enough surprises for one day.

Jake opened his mouth to say something when sounds in the trees had them both ducking and going silent.

Moving back-to-back, they hunted the surrounding jungle. Voices carried to them, from a distance, but getting closer.

"We should go back and check for the bodies," a male voice said. "If they weren't on that boat, what if they got away?"

"They were on the boat and they died," a deeper

male voice said. The man with the deeper voice had a very slight Australian accent.

"We don't even know who *they* were," the first man said.

"Doesn't matter. They stole my yacht. We know there were two of them based on the dive gear. You saw those piles in lifeboat. That was them. No one could have escaped that explosion."

"You're the boss. But given how jumpy Amud is, we shouldn't take any chances."

"Amud got his guns. And we got paid. He's got no reason to worry now."

The first man, who also sounded Australian, snorted. "He always worries. That's the problem doing business with him. Jumpy bastard."

"Enough. We're done here. Let's get off the cursed atoll."

Marta barely breathed as the men walked close enough to where she and Jake crouched among the ferns, she was certain they'd turn their heads and spot them at any moment.

When they were past, and the sounds of them tromping through the undergrowth quieted, she finally let out a breath.

She gave Jake a wide eye look, blew out a relived breath, started to smile…

Then heard a voice with a very distinct Australian accent say, "What've got here now?"

5

Five guys with guns marched Marta and Jake out onto the beach, two of them carrying the golden chest, one lugging their waterproof backpacks with their gear, the other two keeping guns pressed against Marta and Jake's spines so they didn't make a run for it.

Not that there was anywhere to go.

Once they moved out from the shaded humidity of the jungle, the sun was like a punch in the face. Heat stealing her remaining energy, prickling against her already sweat soaked skin. Her t-shirt and running shorts, which had dried from their swim to reach the island, clung to her, sticky and uncomfortable.

Her deck shoes sunk into the soft, hot sand as the gunman behind her nudged her forward, making her stumble. She snarled but didn't say anything. She was too terrified to speak.

Jake stumbled beside her too, using the motion to get closer. "You okay?" he asked.

"Been better."

Two men stood by the small motorboat, watching them approach. And from the jungle behind the two men, another four men emerged.

"Well," the man with the deep voice from the jungle said. "I'm guessing you're not two of Amud's people. Yacht thieves, then?"

The man was a little taller than Marta, with a dark tan that screamed skin cancer to her. His blondish hair was thin and wispy around a wide featured, rough-edged face. His dark sunglasses hid his eyes and reflected the sunlight in little blinding flashes.

"Told you they weren't dead," the other man with him said.

Deep voice gave him a look and he quieted down, staring at the sand.

"I suppose most people in my position would ask *why* you stole my boat. But I think I'm just going to kill you for it and call it a day."

The gun at Marta's back pressed harder into her spine, and she bit her lip to keep from whimpering.

The man glanced around her and Jake to the golden chest. He raised his eyebrows. "Well, I guess I don't have to ask what you're here for after all. Treasure here? How the hell you'd find that?"

"Long story," Jake said.

"Darwinian story," Marta said, a little surprised she could talk.

"Darwin, eh? I'm from Darwin. Shitty place. Prefer my yacht."

"Yeah, sorry about that," Jake said.

"It's alright, mate. You're about to pay me back for it."

"We'd really rather not be shot," Marta said. "You could just…leave us stranded here?"

"Slower death." He nodded. "You'd still die. There's nothing here. Believe me. I've been visiting this little atoll for years now." He gave them both an assessing look. "Suppose a slow death might be a nice sort of revenge, right? Give you hope. Hope's the worst, you know."

His considering look made Marta want to fidget. She kept from tapping her toes by an act of will.

"What's in the chest?" he finally asked.

Jake shrugged. "Didn't get a chance to open it yet. Legend says its cursed. Opening it unleashes the curse. I figured I'd let whoever bought it from me open it."

The smuggler chuckled. "Not as dumb as you look. Curse, you say? Never believed in those much."

He might not, but the other ten men all shuffled a

little more, looking at each other and their feet. The two men carrying the chest exchanged a look, then set it down on the beach a few feet from their boss.

He glanced at it, then looked at Jake. "Open it. Let's see what sort of thing warrants a whole curse."

Jake glanced at Marta. She shook her head. He was making up the part about opening it unleashing the curse. But still, without knowing what was in there, opening it under these circumstances felt overwhelmingly stupid.

Jake pressed his lips together, then knelt down in front of the chest. He stared at it for a long time before he set his hand to the clip.

Noise from the surrounding jungle stopped him midmotion and everyone turned to look.

Another group of men emerged from the palms.

More guns. Marta sighed.

But this group was pointing their guns at the smuggler's group. The smugglers all swung their guns around to point at the new group.

Marta moved closer to Jake now that she no longer had a barrel pressed against her spine.

Jake rose slowly to his feet.

"Amud," the yacht owner said. "What's the problem here?"

Amud motioned to the golden chest. "You've been holding out on me. I don't appreciate that." Amud's accent was a weird blending of South African with just a hint of something Spanish sounding. He was a tall, thin man, wearing tiny rimmed glasses over a sharp nose, his dark hair pulled back into a ponytail longer than Marta's.

"This isn't anything to do with our business," Yacht Owner said.

"Then you won't mind us taking the chest."

"And why would I let you do that?"

"Good will?" Amud shrugged. And more men with guns stepped from the trees, surrounding Yacht Owner's men.

"Too many guns in too small a space," Marta murmured to Jake.

"Yup," he said. They both edged backward, closer to the water.

"We've already established enough good will," Yacht Owner said, "by giving you a fair price on the goods you just bought. The chest is mine."

"I don't think so," Amud said. "That's a lot of gold. Think we'll take that."

Jake and Marta dove behind the cover of the motorboat just as the gunfire started.

6

"Well. This isn't what I expected from this trip," Marta said, wincing as bullets whizzed overhead tunneling into the ocean waves, hissing into the beach and kicking up white sand. "Now what?"

"Don't get shot." Jake chanced a look around the boat, then ducked back quickly when sand puffed at his face from bullets hitting the beach too close to their cover. "Maybe get off this beach."

"Into the water?"

He considered the ocean.

The yacht was still anchored offshore. One smuggler was still aboard, but when Marta and Jake and snuck through the yacht to retrieve their bags and a few other necessaries, the single guard had been sitting in one of the living rooms with a drink in his hand, watching a car race on the big screen TV.

"Can't swim there with the box," he said.

She hated to say this out loud but, "We might have to leave it."

He glanced around the motorboat again.

More bullets whizzed overhead. Shouts and cursing from the beach. Some screaming.

Marta jumped when man hit the ground close to her, his dark sunglasses knocked crooked on his face, his eyes wide open but sightless, blood dripping down his temple.

"Ew." She shivered and looked away.

"Grab his gun," Jake said.

"You remember I'm a terrible shot, right?" Keeping as close to the sand as she could, she stretched out and grabbed the man's long barrel gun, pulling back behind the boat just as a bullet hit the sand near the man.

"Thought your sister was helping you with that," Jake said.

"Apparently, science historians don't need to be good shots." She rolled her eyes.

Jake looked like he might laugh, but more bullets whipped past their scant cover and he winced instead.

Looking around the edge of the boat, he said, "Okay. I want you to cover me. I'm going to get the chest."

"Are you crazy?"

"No point coming all the way out here and leaving it behind."

"So that's a yes, then." She shook her head. "Then what? We can't swim with it."

"Still working on that part." He rose up into a crouch. "Now!"

She came up over the boat firing the stupid gun without actually aiming. The kickback sent her hand flying up and around so the bullets flew everywhere into the already chaotic firefight, despite her best efforts to actual aim.

Jack dove onto the beach, scooting across the sand in a kind of crab crawl that brought him close to the gold chest. He ducked, covering his head as more shots zinged near him, pelting into the sand.

Marta cursed and fired toward the people firing on Jake. Despite her horrendously bad aim, she managed to distract the shooters.

Jake grabbed the chest and pulled it through the sand, scrambling back to cover. He dropped against the side of the motorboat, panting hard, his eyes closed.

"Okay," she said. "Now what?"

"Now…" He opened his eyes and looked around. "Motorboat?"

"It's half grounded. We need to push it back into the water. In the middle of a gun fight?"

She rose up from behind the boat again to fire a few more shots. Then heard the click click of an empty magazine.

"Damn it." She ducked back down as more shots whipped over her head. "There goes our one weapon."

"We need my backpack. It's got the satellite phone."

That was the one thing they hadn't wanted to leave the yacht without. Even if they'd gotten stranded on the atoll, they could have phoned his brother in DC. Help would have arrived eventually.

They both risked a look over and around the boat. The man who'd been holding their backpacks was sprawled in the sand, not moving. The packs were a few feet away from him, but right out in the open.

"I've got no way to distract anyone if you run out there again," she said.

"We need that phone."

"We need to get off this beach."

He stood enough to glance inside the boat, ducking back down before another volley of shots pelted the area around them, digging into the boat.

That wasn't good. They kept hitting the motorboat and at the least it'd be unusable in the water. At worst…

Same thing that happened to the lifeboat.

She did not want to be behind this thing if they hit the engine with those bullets. It might not blow up.

She had no idea if it would or wouldn't. But she didn't want to be sitting right next to the thing when she found out.

"There's a gun inside the boat," he said. "If I can just reach it."

He rose up again, throwing himself over the edge of the boat and scrambling for something. More shots. One hit the boat right next to Jake.

Marta pulled him back down behind cover. "Stop that."

He held up the gun. "Got it. Now cover me."

"Not again." She took the gun from him. Another big one with a long barrel. One day she'd have to learn the difference between these things. She knew enough to find the trigger and turn safeties on and off. This was probably why her sister wouldn't help her learn to shoot better.

She rolled up from behind cover and started shooting randomly into the trees. Most of the beach was empty now, except for the few bodies who hadn't been lucky enough to reach cover in time. That meant most of the firefight was going on inside the trees.

The instant Jake hit the open sand, though, more shots whizzed and zinged past him. She fired in the direction of those shots, heard a scream, winced, and fired more. If she'd actually hit someone it was pure dumb luck.

Jake grabbed his backpack, reached for hers, but

had to pull back and lurch away as more bullets dug into the sand near her bag. He scrambled back to cover, dodging and weaving like a drunk man.

"Get over here," she shouted, waving with the gun, then shooting into the trees again when bullets hit the boat.

Jake fell down next to her, clutching his bag, the chest at his back.

"Don't do that anymore," she said, glaring at him, before firing the last of the bullets in the gun into the trees.

So many bullets.

She tossed the now empty gun back up into the boat.

"Call for help," she said when Jake scooted up so his back was against the hull.

He dug in his bag for the satellite phone, a big gray brick of a thing that looked like it belonged in a different decade. "Even if Rick can send help from nearby, we still have to get off this beach."

The yacht was their only option. But they had to get there. And the only way to do that *with* the chest was the motorboat.

"You call your brother," she said. "I'll get the boat started."

Jake looked at it, looked at her, shook his head, and said, "Help me with the chest first."

They managed to maneuver the chest into the boat

without drawing anymore fire since most of it was concentrated inside the jungle now. From the shouting and yelling, it sounded like the chase was on, people moving deeper into the trees, others following.

She and Jake exchanged a look.

"You push," she said, "I'll get the motor started."

He tossed his backpack and the satellite phone into one of the motorboat's back seats, then boosted her up and over the edge.

She hit the deck with a grunt, then scrambled on her hands and knees to the wheel. The smugglers hadn't bothered to remove the boat's ignition key, which made her life a lot easier.

Though she'd have though, after having one boat stolen already today, the Yacht Owner would have been more careful.

She felt the boat lurch and move and finally catch in the waves, lifting it off the sand. When she was sure they were away from the beach far enough, she started the engine.

Jake's hand appeared at the side of the boat. She leaned over to help pull him, grabbing the back of his shorts and one of his legs in a desperate move to get his heavy ass into the boat.

He hit the deck, wincing. She went back to the wheel and revved the engine, sending the motorboat lurching in a wide circle until they were charging fast across the waves.

Jake dropped into the co-pilot's seat with the satellite phone in hand.

They circled to the far side of the yacht as he made his call. By the time they reached the swim platform, he'd finished. He roped the motorboat to the yacht long enough for them to scramble both the chest and his pack back aboard. Once she was on the yacht, he removed the rope and pushed the boat away.

"That's our only escape if the guy that's still on here objects to our presence," she said.

"I'm sure we can come to an understanding."

TURNED OUT THE REMAINING GUARD HAD HEARD THE gunfight on the beach and had already been debating abandoning his boss and the others. He wasn't particularly loyal. So he was perfectly willing to accept Jake's alternative offer.

Granted, Jake made his alternative offer at gunpoint since they'd found another one in the motorboat. The gun was just the extra bit of incentive the smuggler needed.

With the smuggler happily tied up in the living room with the big screen TV, Jake and Marta sat on the bridge, Jake in the captain's seat, the yacht heading back toward Tahiti.

They'd only been underway for fifteen minutes

when they saw the military helicopters buzz by, heading toward the atoll.

"Rick's backup?" she asked, watching the green camouflage painted choppers pass.

"Rick's backup," Jake said.

"All right. He can date my sister." She smiled. And patted the golden chest where it sat between them.

"You want to open it before we get back?" he asked, glancing down at it.

She shook her head. "Let's wait until we're somewhere safe."

He raised his brows in questions.

"Just in case there is a curse." She shrugged. "I think we've had enough 'luck' already."

Taking the Heat

1

Andy climbed out of her Jeep, jumped up onto the running board, and grabbing the roll bar for balance while she scanned the two-lane highway.

Behind her, a line of stopped cars stretched as far back as she could see. Radio claimed the backup went on for miles. To the east, the ominous black clouds of the forest fire causing this mass evacuation darkened the sky.

The highway was bracketed by pines, but the normally nice smell got swamped beneath the hot tarmac and car stench, with the distant taste of smoke. So far, the wind worked in their favor, keeping the fire away from the evacuation route. But too many cars combined with the inevitable chaos had resulted in an accident two miles ahead. Stopped traffic for the last forty-five minutes. And no way off the highway that didn't lead toward the fire.

She rubbed her arm across her forehead, swiping at the sweat trickling into her eyes. Hot as a bear's butt, muggy, and the flavor of smoke. Made the delay a lot worse. All the cars around her had their engines off, and half of the people had gotten out, standing near or leaning on their cars, watching the parked vehicles ahead of them in the distance. Everyone waiting for the flash of brake lights and the first creep of movement.

When traffic had stopped, and not moved for fifteen minutes, with no cars coming from the opposite direction, people had started trying to get out of the block by driving up the wrong side of the highway. Which only got that side blocked up, too. There was no turning around and going back the way she'd come. There wasn't even any room for emergency vehicles from behind them to reach the wreck. And with the sun lowering toward the horizon, the red glow of the distant fire was coming into view.

What a disaster.

Andy sighed and leaned against the roll bar on top of her open-sided Jeep.

CB radio chatter from the truck behind her caught her attention.

"Nothing's moving. Can't get through. Too far back."

Andy nodded to the man listening to the CB. "What's happening?" she called.

The man, late sixties, cowboy hat set low on his forehead, carried his CB with him from his truck when he ambled over to join her.

"Listening to the crews working the fire," he said. "Sounds like they're short pilots for a support run and the ground crew is gonna be in trouble soon without more backup."

"Doesn't sound good. They have fresh pilots on the way?"

He nodded back over his shoulder. "The pilots that were called in to help are stuck about ten, fifteen miles back in this mess with no way through." He pushed his hat back on his head, squinting at the traffic. Sweat trickled down his brown cheek. "The highway patrol got called to make a path for them, but between the block and the accident, they're stretched and nothing's moving."

Several more people from the surrounding cars moved toward Andy's Jeep. "They can't get planes from somewhere else to fly in?" one man asked.

"Sounds like it's not the planes that are the problem. Got enough of those. Just need one or two more pilots," the older man said.

"Whole region is stretched thin," a woman said. She rubbed a bandana across the back of her neck, lifting her heavy black braid. "Heard there aren't enough firefighters or pilots anywhere."

"Got a ground crew in the area about to be in trouble," the older man said. "Not too far from here."

"Shit," a young man with a cane said. He'd come from a car farther ahead of Andy's. "Just heard on the weather report, they're worried about the wind shifting."

A middle-aged woman with a fussy toddler on her hip looked up from cooing at her kid. "Are we in trouble here?"

"Not as far as I can tell," the young man said. "It's the ground crews that'll be in trouble if the wind changes."

"And help trapped in the snarl," the older man with the CB radio said.

"How far away is the airstrip from here?" Andy asked, frowning at the surrounding trees. "Anyone know?"

Lot of head shaking and passed looks.

"Not sure exactly," the older man said. "Turn offs about a mile ahead though. Maybe…three miles as the crow flies."

She nodded, her gaze narrowed. She could probably get there within the hour, so long as the older man's estimate wasn't too far off. She'd have to stick to the roads. If she knew where she was going, even the right direction, she could cut through the woods.

But without a location, and with the unpredictability of the fire… No. Couldn't help anyone if she got herself lost in the woods.

Stepping off the running board, she said, "I'm gonna move my Jeep as far over as I can get it. Should give you enough room if traffic gets moving again."

"Where you going?" the older man asked, frowning.

"Figure I can find the airstrip in an hour if I stick to the roads. If the jam breaks and the pilots back there can get through, the more the merrier."

"You a pilot."

She nodded. She didn't miss the stares and pauses, the small group waiting for her to elaborate. She didn't.

"Gonna be a hike," the woman with the toddler said.

"I'll manage." She gave the little kid a smile and a finger wave before she got into her Jeep and pulled it as far off the road as the trees allowed. Far enough she had to get out on the passenger side.

She reached into the back seat for the small backpack that served as her suitcase and purse all in one, slinging it over her shoulders.

The older man said, "Sounds like they still aren't having any luck getting through." He gave her a look. "You sure about this?"

"I'm sure. Good luck. Stay safe."

He nodded and tipped his cowboy hat at her. Which made her smile.

The woman with the thick braid tossed her a bottle of water. Andy caught it easily.

"You're going to need that," the woman said.

"Thanks." She raised the bottle to the small group. Then headed up the side of the road, skirting the edge of the parking lot the highway had become.

2

She reached the airstrip a half hour later, jogging the length of the side road once she reached it. The air was thick and muggy, the smell of distant smoke still coating her tongue. But around the airfield, the sky was clear, bright and sunny, the shadows lengthening beneath the tall pines.

A plane was just taking off as she reached the ground control center, the rush of air cooling the sweat on her head and neck. A DC-10, Very Large Airtanker, that could carry upward of eight thousand gallons of fire retardant. Big mother that required two people to fly it, but could cover a sizable chunk of ground.

Just couldn't get too low or maneuver into tight areas.

Three other smaller planes sat to the edge of the runway. Two AT-802F Fire Bosses and a CL-415 from what she could see. Great water scoopers for tighter runs and could carry between eight hundred and sixteen hundred gallons of water. Ground crews scrambled around them.

The organized chaos, the smell of jet fuel, the heat and noise…brought her back. Maybe a little too familiar. Too comfortable.

Memories of the last time she'd been at an airfield knocked on the door she'd locked them behind. She ignored the knock and headed into the office beneath the flight tower.

The chaos was more obvious here. People on phones and radios, all talking at once. Maps spread over tables with people arguing and poking at various spots on the map. Screens pinging. Calls down from the tower above. And when she glanced back outside, she saw a Fire Boss on final approach. The wings wobbled in a cross breeze, dipping dangerously.

"She's coming in hard," Andy called into the noise.

Two of the people arguing at the table over the paper map rushed to the door. The woman pulled a radio from her vest pocket and shouted into it, scrambling the emergency crew. The man rushed up the stairs into the tower.

As Andy watched from the doorway, the plane's wings continued to dip and dive, the plane dancing sideways, its nose rising too high, then dipping too low as it descended too fast.

"Shit," the woman who'd been shouting into the radio muttered. "She's not gonna make it."

A tense silence gathered between Andy and the woman. And Andy found herself trying to coach the pilot in her head. "Little bit slower, back on the stick, nose up, gotta take down the speed..." She didn't open her mouth, but the old litany rolled through her mind. The familiar tightening in her gut. Those memories knocked louder against the locked door.

The plane hit the runway hard, bounced, hit again, and the pilot lost the nose. It dipped low, hit the ground, and sent the plane sideways, one wing breaking against the black tarmac.

Emergency crews rushed toward the plane before it fully settled, some held hoses spraying water over the smoking engine as others scrambled to pull the pilot from the wreck.

Andy held perfectly still until the memories stopped knocking. Until the pilot emerged from the still intact flight deck and shakily climbed down the later. EMTs circled him, but the pilot walked away on his own legs.

"I'll take it," the woman next to Andy said quietly, echoing Andy's thoughts.

Finally, when it was clear the pilot was fine and

the plane wasn't going to catch fire, the woman turned to face Andy. "Who're you?"

"Andy MacDermott. Heard you were short pilots. I was closer than the ones caught farther back in the road block. Thought I'd see if I could help."

"Rating?"

Andy gave an abbreviated rundown of her flight experience, the over four thousand flight hours, eight hundred flight instructor hours, limited fifty hours in seaplanes, five hundred hours low-level flight... She wanted to leave off the part that got the most questions but included it for the sake of assuring the woman she could handle the crafts they had sitting outside, even though she'd never flown those exact models.

"Before retiring, I was an instructor at Edwards Air Force Base. TPS."

"Test Pilot School, huh?" The woman narrowed her eyes. She was maybe mid-fifties, her red hair streaked with silver, pulled back in a no-nonsense bun under her Fire Rangers hat, her pale skin dotted with freckles. She had that hard stare that investigated souls before making decisions.

Andy liked her immediately.

"Brenda Cowls. Fire chief. You think you can handle one of the 802s?"

"Figure I can manage."

"Good." Brenda took a note handed to her by a

young man who scurried away a second later. She glanced at the paper, then folded it very precisely. "Everyone on the mountain is stretched thin." She gestured at the wreck. "Pilots we have are flying too long. Getting tired, getting sloppy. Conditions are too difficult for fatigued crew. And I have a group on the east ridge in danger of getting trapped within the hour if we can't get them more support. The angle is tough. The smoke is thick. We haven't been able to cover enough ground to give them room." She sighed and tapped the folded paper against her thigh. "No one else can spare any pilots. And the couple we've been able to find in the area are stuck in traffic." She met Andy's gaze. "Situation is changing fast. And I don't have the crew to handle it."

"I'll do what I can. I'm fresh. I can give you some time to get the others here."

"Never done drop runs, though."

"Not fire," she confirmed. "But I did some crop dusting in my youth."

Brenda huffed. "That'll do. Not a lot of options." She muttered a curse under her breath. "We fuck this up, those fighters are dead."

"I'll get them the cover they need."

And she would. She refused to fail anyone who needed her help again.

3

By the time the runway was cleared, Andy was up to speed on the surroundings and situation. She got her bearings on the map, and a quick run down from Brenda on the plane she'd be flying.

"Remember, as you drop all that weight, push full forward stick or risk a stall. You crash this plane, we don't have a replacement in the area. And we already lost one today. You have to be at sixty feet above the treetops before you drop, or it'll just evaporate in mid-air, waste everyone's time, resources, and probably kill the ground crew."

"So," Andy said as she ran through her preflight checks, "no pressure then."

"Just life or death," Brenda said with a nod. "Ordinary day."

Andy flashed her a small smile. "I got this."

Brenda gave her one last look. Then, "I'll stay in the tower and guide you through it. Remember you've only got this one shot. Even if you had experience scooping, by the time you get to the nearest lake and back, it'll be too late."

Andy nodded. Brenda tapped the edge of the flight deck, then scurried back down the later as Andy closed the door.

For a heartbeat, Andy let being inside a cockpit again really sink in. The feel of the leather seat. The faint smell of fuel and engine grease. The instruments coming online. The snug hold of the harness securing her in her seat.

Home.

As she took hold of the stick and taxied to the runway, she let it all flow back to her. The remembered feel of the plane's vibrations, the sense of the wind and gusts against the hull. Not the same, exactly. She'd never flown this exact type of plane. But that hardly mattered to her memories.

She got clearance, powered down the runway, and launched into the sky like she'd never left. The wings dipped a little as she caught a cross breeze and she had to wrestle the thing back to rights. But it only took a few minutes to get a feel for the craft. Not a jet fighter. Not any of the experimental planes she'd tested over the years. Not the training planes she'd used to teach students. But the feeling of being in the air again, of being in control of her fate hadn't changed.

And it felt damned good.

Now she had some firefighters to save.

THE FIRE TURNED THE SKY RED. EVERYTHING AROUND her glowing. Black smoke blotting out the blue skies. Smoke and burnt wood thick on her tongue, making her eyes burn. The heat, even at this height, intense. Sweat trickled down her temples.

She'd flown over the area twice, confirming there were no obstacles, confirming the location of the ground crew. Everything was clear. She was ready.

"Adjust heading," Brenda's voice over the radio. "Almost there. Remember you have to be at sixty feet for this to work."

"Right, Tower. Starting my run."

The lower she got the plane, the harder it got to control. Crosswinds and heat currents tugged and pulled at the plane until it felt like it was going to rip apart.

She couldn't even see the ground crew from this angle anymore. Had to hope they hadn't moved since her last lap around.

"Still too high," Brenda warned. "Gotta get down more."

Down more put her right on top of burning trees. Heat pockets and currents kept pushing the plane higher. Like forcing her way through mud to get the plane to the right altitude.

To the east, a burning pine exploded, the sound and wash of heat hitting her at once, wobbling the plane and her nerves. If one of these things exploded beneath her, they were all screwed.

"Gotta get lower," Brenda warned again.

Andy put all her strength into forcing the plane lower, forcing it past those pockets of hot air trying to drive her back into the sky, or suck her under and flip her into the burning trees.

She didn't dare take her hands off the wheel to wipe away the sweat dripping down her face. Blinked hard to clear her vision.

"Almost there," Brenda said. "Adjust your angle."

Andy counted down in her head, her gaze jumping between her instruments and the raging fire ahead. The heat sucked out all the oxygen. She gritted her teeth. Reached one.

Dropped her load.

The full tanks of water swept out behind and below her, covering a swath of the fire and dousing a small section to leave a clear path for the firefighters.

Over the radio, Andy heard the tower cheering.

"Dead on," Brenda said. "Ground crew reporting they've got room to breathe."

Andy fought the little plane, now considerably lighter, forcing it back up to a safer altitude. Through gritted teeth, she said, "Roger that, Tower. Glad it worked."

"Up for another run?" Brenda asked.

Still struggling with control of the plane, Andy said, "Sure."

She jumped and jostled back into the sky, until she broke free of the fire's grabby currents. Then turned the plane back toward the airfield. If she'd been trained to this, Brenda had told her there was a lake not too far away she could have scooped up more water into the tanks beneath the plane. But without even a practice run at that, they hadn't wanted to risk it.

As she cleared the worst of the fire, though, heading back toward safer ground, something in the trees caught her attention. She banked low, swinging over the tops of still unharmed pine.

And spotted the truck with someone standing in the bed waving up at her.

"Tower, I've got someone in need of help here." She glanced at her instruments and reported the coordinates. "Got anyone in the area."

She banked over the trees to make another pass over the truck. Her fuel gage showed enough to make it back to the landing strip plus enough for an extra few passes over the truck. But not enough to stay in the area until help arrived.

"No one that isn't needed for the fire," Brenda said. "Are they in the fire's path?"

Andy did another higher circle of the surroundings. "Worst of it's to the southwest. Winds blowing it away. If that shifts, though, they're right in the line."

Silence over the radio. Andy did another slow circle over the surroundings. About a mile from the truck, she spotted a lake. The lake Brenda had mentioned was in the area. Not huge. But long enough to land on.

She hadn't done a water landing in years. But she'd done them.

She took one more pass over the stranded man. This time she spotted the kid standing next to the truck as the man continued to wave frantically up at her.

This wasn't a passenger plane. There wasn't a lot of wiggle room in the cockpit. She had the fuel. But squeezing three people in a space designed for one...

"Anyone near enough to get to them?" She radioed again.

Brenda finally came back to her. "Not for at least a half hour. And looks like the winds are shifting."

Fuck. "I'm landing on this lake up here. I'll get them out."

"They aren't going to fit in that plane."

"I'll make it work."

She angled around until she had the plane lined up with the water.

"When was the last time you landed on water?" Brenda said, her voice steady and even. All business.

"Been a few years."

"Keep the nose higher than you think it needs to be," Brenda said, quietly coaching Andy through the process. Step by step. Andy glided down to the water, skimming the surface, letting the pontoons touch down. The stick bucked in her hands but she gripped tight and kept the nose and wings from dipping.

It wasn't butter. But she made the landing without breaking apart the plane, so she'd take it.

"Thanks for talking me through that," she said to Brenda as she motored the plane to a wide bank, wide enough to hold most of the plane. "I'll radio once I've got everyone."

"There's a first aid kit and fire blankets in the plane. Take those with you."

"Got 'em. Out." She grabbed the blankets and kit, all of which were small enough she could still jog with them, then climbed down from the plane.

She got her bearings, studying the surroundings, the angle of the sun. Getting lower in the sky. The red glow of the fire to the southwest seemed brighter now. The taste of smoke still coated her tongue. Sweat trickled down her back. She swiped a hand across her forehead, pushing her hair back up into her loosened bun. Then took off at a steady jog through the pines in the direction of the truck.

4

I t took Andy a solid ten minutes to reach them. This part of the forest was still untouched by the fire, but the dirt road she found curved toward the fire's path. Unless it turned again, no one was driving out of here in that direction.

When she reached the truck, she got a better view of the problem. A huge downed pine covered the road in the direction leading away from the fire.

"You folks need some help?" she asked as she got close enough to be heard.

The man in the back of the truck looked to be in his late sixties maybe. Gray hair under a gray baseball cap. Face a little weathered. He climbed carefully out of the truck bed. The kid Andy had spotted from above came around to stand just behind the older man. Probably no more than ten, maybe a tall eight given how young he looked. He clutched the man's hand when the man reached for him.

"Sure could," the man said. "My grandson and I got trapped trying to get out of the area." He nodded at the downed tree. "I got a small ax, but it's not making a dent in that tree fast enough. Hoped that plane spotted me."

"There's a lake about a mile back. Plane's there. Winds shifted, so I don't think we'll have time to chop through the tree."

"Grandpa?" The boy's voice shook.

The man patted his shoulder. "Grab your croc," he said. "We'll head out."

The boy rushed to the truck.

"Name's James," the man said, extending a hand. "My grandson is Ben."

"Andy." She shook his hand. When Ben came back around the side of the truck clutching a huge stuffed crocodile, Andy smiled. "Like your friend there."

"We have to save him, too," Ben said.

"Of course we do." To James, she said, "We can't take too much. Not sure I can squeeze you into the plane nonetheless any gear. But anything irreplaceable, grab it now."

James put an arm around his grandson and patted the pocket of his cargo pants with his free hand, where she assumed he had his wallet. "Got everything I need right here."

Ben lifted his crocodile. "Me too."

"All right then. Follow me."

THE HIKE BACK WENT A LITTLE SLOWER THAN ANDY'S trip to the truck. James and Ben were fit enough for the part of the trek once they got off the smooth dirt road, but the setting sun left the area under the trees dark and precarious. Last thing they needed was someone spraining an ankle or, worse, breaking a bone.

The smell of smoke got stronger with the shifting winds, the acrid tang raising Andy's tension. And from the tightening around James' mouth, he was worried too.

She kept most of her focus on making sure she got the two back to the lake without getting lost in the unfamiliar territory. She'd marked her path using a pair of scissors from the first aid kit to dig shallow gouges into large trees. But the marks got harder to see the darker it got.

And as the light faded, the sky overhead turned redder, the fire glow closer than it had been when Andy landed.

"What were you two doing before the evacuation

started?" Andy asked, hoping a little conversation might help.

"Grandpa and I were fishing in his summer cabin," Ben said.

"You fish *inside* a cabin?" Andy feigned shock. "Wow, that's impressive."

Ben laughed. "Not *inside* the cabin," he drawled.

"Yeah, that's for winter fishing, right?" James said.

Ben snorted. "Momma doesn't like that kind of fishing. She says it's too cold."

"My daughter-in-law's more of a city girl," James said with fondness.

"We were river fishing," Ben said. "Catching trite."

"Trout," James corrected gently.

"Trout," Ben said. "And Howard promised not to eat them."

"Howard?" Was there someone else trapped they needed to find?

"My crocodile," Ben said.

Ah. Well, they were already rescuing Howard.

"He likes fish," Ben said.

"Where'd he get a name like Howard?" She spotted another of her marks and angled her little group slightly to follow the path.

In the distance, she caught the faint sounds of the fire crackling and popping through the trees. But closer, the slush of water against shore. Almost there.

"He's never told me," Ben said. "Just that his name was Howard."

"Fair enough. Does Howard fish too, or just watch."

"He fishes too, but he's lazy. He waits for me to reel the fish in."

She kept up the questions about Howard and fishing for another few minutes. It was nearly full dark by then and she could no longer spot the cuts she'd made in the trees. But that faint shooshing sound of water got her the rest of the way.

They broke from the trees farther down the bank from the plane than where she'd gone in. But the plane was still there.

The sky overhead was even redder once they moved out from under the forest canopy. And thick black clouds of smoke swam in the air a few miles away.

James let out a low whistle. "That's closer than I expected." His voice shook a little.

Ben tightened his hold on Howard and grabbed his grandfather's hand again.

"Plane's waiting," she said, trying to draw their attention away from the approaching fire.

They all jogged the last few yards.

"Okay, this is going to be a tight squeeze." She

directed most of her instructions to Ben. You'll need to hold Howard tight and squeeze in just behind the pilot's seat. There's just enough room there for the two of you. James, I apologize for this ahead of time, but I'll need to sit in your lap. This will be awkward and a little difficult, but I'll get us back to the landing field. Okay?"

James held her gaze, then looked at the fire, then down at his grandson. "Okay, buddy, let's go."

James climbed into the plane first. Andy left the first aid kid and fire blankets on the shore, so Ben would have room behind the seat where the gear had been stored. She handed him and Howard up the ladder to James, who got him squeezed into the narrow nook behind the seat. Once Ben was settled, she climbed up and awkwardly climbed onto James' lap, sitting between his legs as best she could. The position put her too far forward. It was going to make flying really tricky. But better this than leaving them behind.

"Sorry for the tight space," she said. Switching on the engine, a brief moment of sputtering worry, and then the engines caught and whirled to life. "Hold on tight."

She dropped the headset over her ears and radioed the tower. "Got two new passengers—"

"Three!" Ben said.

"Sorry, two humans and a crocodile. Ready to head back, Tower. How's it looking?"

"Fire's moved closer to your location," someone who wasn't Brenda answered. He gave her new flight coordinates to get her back to the strip. "How's your fuel?"

She considered her gages as she puttered the plane onto the lake, lining it up so she had enough room for a takeoff, and made a rough mental calculation with the added passenger weight but no water in the hold and taking the altered flight plan into consideration.

"It'll get us back," she said. Might be close. But they'd get there. Even if she had to glide them in on fumes.

Tower acknowledged.

Andy shouted to Ben and James over the engine noise, "Here we go. Hold on to your stomachs."

She gunned the little plane, and it skimmed across the water, launching into the air just as the far shore approached. Ben shouted in triumph, which made Andy grin.

"Don't worry, Howard," Ben told his stuffed crocodile. "We'll be safe soon."

"Be back on the ground and safe before you know it," she assured.

And turned the plane toward the airstrip, the fire's red glow bright behind her.

5

Andy radioed in the names of her two accidental passengers, and the contact details for Ben's mom so she'd know her family was safe. Crosswinds on the landing at the airstrip made getting the little plane down tricky, but the extra passenger weight helped. The fuel gage was yelling at her on finally approach, but there was just enough to get them through the landing. The engines sputtered and died before she could taxi the plane to the refueling area, though, so it needed a tow to get it out of the way.

The airfield, lit by bright halogen lamps, still teamed with chaos, coming and going, another support plane taking off the minute Andy's plane was out of the way. And another plane lined up and took off minutes after that. The whoosh and roar of the small planes, the darkness, the shouted sounds of ground crew… So familiar. Even if it had been a long time.

She got James and Ben to the offices, where Brenda and a young man, who turned out to be an EMT, waited. The young man whisked James and Ben off for a quick exam, to ensure no injuries or damage from smoke inhalation—despite James protests that they were both fine. But Ben wanted Howard the crocodile examined for injuries, and the EMT agreed that was a good idea, so James relented.

Before they left though, James clasped Andy's hand, giving it a hard shake. "Thanks for getting us out. I can't thank you enough."

"Not necessary. I'm glad you and Ben are safe."

"And Howard," Ben said.

"And Howard," Andy added.

James gave her a little wink, then followed the young medic to a side office Andy assumed was an exam room.

"Wouldn't have recommended the side trip," Brenda said, her gaze on the closed exam room door. "But glad you did it."

"Me too." She faced Brenda. "Still need me to make another run?" Even as she asked, the roar of a third plane taking off rumbled the windows.

"Road block cleared and our three backup pilots made it in. Could always use more help. But we're good now." She nodded at the closed door. "You've had an eventful night."

"Did you reach the mother?"

"She's on the way. Be here in probably another hour."

"They good to wait here?"

"Sure. I think I can scrape up some crocodile food somewhere around here."

Andy chuckled. "Since you've got the qualified people here now, I'll leave the work to the experts. I have a retirement party to get to in San Diego."

Brenda nodded, and somewhat to Andy's surprise, didn't ask any follow up questions. "I assume you wouldn't turn down a ride back to your car?"

"You'd assume correctly."

Brenda smiled, a gentle look that didn't last long, and signaled to one of the people standing over the giant paper map. "Devon here will get you back." She stretched out a hand. "Thanks again. For everything. Saved some lives today."

Andy returned the woman's handshake firmly, and forced down the memories of the lives she hadn't saved. Maybe this helped make up for it. At least a little.

"Enjoy the retirement party," Brenda said. "Stay safe out there."

"You too." Andy gave her a look as Brenda handed her back her backpack.

"I'm not the one flying over the tops of burning trees anymore. But I'll pass your well wishes on to the pilots that are."

The ride back to her Jeep took a lot less time than her jog up to the airfield. As Brenda had said, the roadblock had cleared and there were only a few cars passing on the way out of the area. No one on the side heading toward the fire.

Her Jeep was where she'd left it. She was a little surprised to find a note on the windshield from the older man who'd had the CB radio, telling her he'd waited by her car until the traffic had all cleared off, and he hoped everything had worked out. His name was also Ben. She smiled and tucked the note into her backpack.

Behind the wheel, the engine quietly humming, she considered her destination. She'd been dreading the retirement party for her former commander. She hadn't seen him since she left the Air Force, since she'd lost two students during a test flight and hadn't felt she could continue teaching. The mistakes weren't hers directly, but she'd still felt responsible.

Being inside a plane again today had brought back a lot of the old feelings. The guilt. But also the rush of taking control and doing what she knew she was capable of doing.

Colonel Avery had tried to talk her out of taking early retirement and leaving the Air Force all those years ago. He'd accused her of quitting. Of walking away.

She didn't walk away today.

She'd wanted to make his party—he'd been her biggest mentor—but she hadn't wanted to face the past, or rehash old arguments.

But maybe there didn't have to be arguments. Maybe she could forgive herself the lost lives finally.

She pulled the Jeep back up onto the road and headed south. She had a party to make.

And some past mistakes to forgive along the way.

Deadly Breaks

1

Connor adjusted his pen light, shining it more fully onto the stubborn bar lock pinned across the thick metal door. Around him night bugs chirped, a pine-scented breeze blew across his overheated cheeks, the deep shadows swayed as clouds churned past overhead. The fresh, clean air carried just a hint of salt water from the ocean, not more than a half mile away.

Quiet, peaceful, serene.

It was fucking awful.

A mosquito buzzed his cheek. He slapped the bastard away. He hated nature. Nature sucked.

He was going to kill Howards.

He glanced behind him, checking the line of pines across the length of the tarmacked parking lot. Outside of his rented SUV parked in the darker shadows next to the square brick building holding the toilets, there were no other cars or trucks in the lot. The rest stop was deep enough into the National Park, he couldn't even hear traffic from the distant highway.

No one bearing down on him. Yet.

At least he hoped no one was hiding in the trees. Fuck if he'd know. Give him a city alley. A concrete jungle. The back alleys of Prague. The sewers beneath the London Underground. Skyscrapers in Hong Kong.

He could tell you which window some bastard was looking out staring down at him from eight stories up.

But set him into the middle of a National Park along the Washington coast…

He snarled and put the pen light between his teeth to hold it on the lock, freeing up both hands. Who the fuck put a bar lock across a rest stop toilet door anyway? And not just any bar lock. No. This one had to be the hardest fucking lock to pick in the history of locks.

His heartbeat pounded as something hooted overhead. Could be a bird. Could be messages sent between the assholes trying to stop him.

More hooting.

If that was a fucking owl, he was going to shoot it.

"Two days tops, Howards says," he muttered around the pen light as he adjusted the picks in the lock, trying to hit the little catch inside. "Easy work, he says."

Easy work, his ass. Who the hell hides anything of value in a public toilet at a rest stop in the middle of nowhere?

Connor glanced at the large blue Porta Potties. Three of them in a row right next to the brick toilet building.

He supposed the hiding place could have been worse.

Thankfully the breeze was blowing away from the Porta Potties. Pine trees were bad enough. He could do without the extra ambiance of unemptied temp toilets.

Rubbing a hand across his face, trying to swipe away sweat, he let out a slow breath. Steady hands. He needed steady hands or this wouldn't work.

He took hold of the two thin metal picks and twisted, turned.

Crunch.

Steps on the rough gravel between the parking lot and the building.

Connor stilled, hoping he blended into the shadows in his black clothing. The hood on his hoodie was up over his head hiding his hair and hopefully masking the light from his mini flashlight. His black gloves kept his hands hidden.

Crunch.

Closer now.

The hairs on his neck stood up. Someone standing right behind him.

He turned slowly, knowing he was going to see a gun pointed at his head.

"Horrrrnk."

Conor blinked as hot air, spit, and animal musk blasted him in the face.

Not a gun.

A moose. A moose the size of a fucking bus.

The animal snorted puffs of hot, musty air into his face again.

Connor had to look a long way up from his crouched position to see the big, thick antlers on that moose's head.

"Never seen a moose in person before," he murmured, slowly taking the penlight from his mouth and flicking the light off. Could moose see in the dark?

Must or the stupid giant thing wouldn't be standing there staring at him.

"Good moose," he said. "Good moose. I'm just going to stand up now."

He rose slowly, holding his hands out, letting the moose see he wasn't holding any weapons. Because a moose would care about that shit? He had no idea. He wasn't an animal guy.

The moose snorted and released another, "Horrrnk."

Connor winced. Ouch. This guy could silence Times Square with that noise.

"Okay," he said to the moose. "I got to get into this john. And I need to do it soon. There's some bad guys out in those woods somewhere. And if they get here before I break into that door, there's gonna be a whole mess of trouble. Right? So if you wouldn't mind just…" He made a shooing motion with his hands.

Moose stomped a foot and huffed in his face again.

"You could do with some toothpaste, big guy," he muttered.

He took a single step backward, away from Moose. Moose took a step toward him.

Yeah, that wasn't going to be good.

He let out a sigh and reached for his gun, tucked up under his hoodie in his shoulder harness. He kept his movements slow. Getting trampled in the middle of nowhere by a prehistoric animal while reaching for his gun was not what he wanted written into his obituary.

As slowly as he'd reached into his heavy hoodie, he moved the gun out, his gaze steady on Moose.

His gun had barely cleared the zipper, when he heard a very feminine throat clearing.

"I hope you don't intend on shooting that animal. It's protected."

He turned to face the woman while mentally cursing Howards into the fourth circle of Hell.

She stood a few feet away, near the building like she'd just walked around it. Dressed in green khaki pants and a loose dark jacket with a circular patch on the chest. She had a green, felt park ranger's hat covering what looked like dark hair, and a very prominent weapon in a side holster on her hip.

So he probably shouldn't antagonize her or mention she was really pretty even with the ugly hat.

Good to know. Good to know.

"Wasn't gonna shoot him," he said, speaking as slowly and calmly to the ranger as he'd spoken to Moose. "Was just going to fire a shot at the trees and scare him away."

"That's a good way to get trampled," she said. Her gaze moved between Moose and Connor, her hand near her belt. "I'd suggest walking very slowly toward me and we'll get into my truck until he leaves."

She had a truck? How the hell had he missed a truck rolling into the rest stop?

"That'd be a good plan, but Moose here seems to want to follow where I go."

"You carrying moose snacks?"

He frowned at her. "What the hell are moose snacks?"

"A joke, city boy." She jerked her chin. "This way. And maybe put that gun away."

He looked back at Moose. Moose snorted more fetid air in his face. He didn't put his gun away.

"You heard the lady," he said. "Just gonna go right over there. No reason to get upset, right?"

Once Moose was gone, he'd figure out a way to get the ranger to leave the area. Then he could go back to lock picking. But he was running out of time, and the ticking clock in his head was starting to speed up. He hadn't been all that far ahead of Schmidt.

The minute he edged toward the ranger, Moose stomped his huge foot and horrrnked again.

"Told you," Connor said. "Seems to want me to stay right here."

"Right there you're a sitting duck."

"Yup. Aware of that. Not sure how to get out of it."

She looked behind him, then cursed under her breath. "Forgot about that stupid lock."

"Yeah, it's not budging either." He winced. Moose had him off is game. Well Moose and all those damned trees. Telling a law-abiding ranger he'd been trying to pick the bathroom lock was a mistake.

"The other side is open," she said. "If we can get around the corner, we can at least wait him out somewhere strong enough he can't knock it over."

The other side was open.

Connor edged closer to the ranger again. Moose

huffed and took a shuffling step forward, crowding Connor against the wall.

"You sure I can't shoot him?" he asked the ranger.

"You can, but you'll just piss him off. Also, I'll have to charge your dead body with shooting a protected species inside the park."

"Fair enough." He was still tempted. Not that he wanted to piss Moose off. But he really needed to get both Moose and Ranger out of here.

Another hooting noise echoed across the rest stop parking lot.

He closed his eyes briefly. That was definitely not an owl.

The first bullet hit a cement block on the bathroom right next to Connor's cheek.

2

Connor dove for cover, wrapping an arm around the ranger and taking her with him as he charged around the corner of the rest stop bathroom. Another chunk of cement zinged off a building block, catching him across the ear.

Moose bellowed, loud enough to make Connor wince. But he didn't have time to see if the beast had taken a hit or was just mad.

"Inside," the ranger shouted.

"We'll be trapped, we go in there."

"Better than standing out here and getting shot."

True. But the bathroom was a solid square of cement blocks with only tiny windows up high and a metal door that, while solid, wouldn't keep Schmitt and his crew out long.

"You have a truck?" he said. "How far?"

"Too far." She nodded.

A dark green four-by-four sat two hundred yards across wide open ground, at the opposite side of another chunk of parking lot.

"How'd you think we'd reach that before Moose charged?" he asked, shaking his head.

"Didn't think the moose would charge us." More gun shots. Ranger winced. "Who the hell is shooting at us? Those aren't rifles they're using. Not illegal hunting."

Illegal maybe, but not the kind of hunting she was thinking about. "The bad guys," he said. "And they're very motivated to keep me from getting something inside the locked portion of this bathroom."

"What and why and who are you?"

"Lot to explain. No time to do it."

No intention of explaining fully. They could argue about that later.

More gun fire. Both he and Ranger ducked as one of the bullets shattered glass on the other side of the building. One of the high windows.

"How many?" she asked.

He glanced at her long enough to see she'd pulled the handgun from her holster. He might be starting to like Ranger. "What's your name?"

"Joy."

"A park ranger named Joy?"

"You make fun of my name right now, I'm gonna let Moose have you."

"If the guns haven't got him." Poor Moose. "My guess would be there are five of them. But that's a guess based on hours old information. Could be more by now."

"If I'm last-standing with someone, I should know his name, too."

"Connor. It's a pleasure to meet you, Joy."

He risked a look around the building. Two men were walking across the open lot toward the bathroom. Too dark to see who they were. But since neither of them was over six foot seven, he knew Schmitt was still somewhere in the trees.

He leaned back against the concrete. "You gonna shoot me if I kill some bad guys?"

"No. But I'm gonna have questions after."

"Fair enough." He swung around the building again, taking aim, and fired four shots.

He missed one of the men completely when he dove to the ground, but he caught the second. The man dropped backward, landing with a clatter on the tarmac.

Some shouting from the trees and another volley of bullets rained down on the bathroom.

They were going to figure out they could circle around soon. If they weren't doing that already.

Connor scanned the lot. Outside of a few tiny trees

planted in spots of grass that served as dividers between sections of the lot, there was no cover close enough to help them out of this.

Moose bellowed again. So not dead. Connor's relief surprised him a little.

More shouting from the trees.

He risked a glance around the corner. He couldn't see Moose, but the guy he'd missed was scrambling back to the trees, fast. The guy he'd shot was still sprawled on the ground.

A few more rounds from the trees. And then silence descended.

Yeah. He didn't trust that silence at all.

"They're going to circle around," Ranger Joy said.

"Yup."

"Your vehicle?"

His rental SUV was parked on the other side of the building, closer to the trees. They might be able to make it and make a run for it. That would get Joy out of here. But it would leave behind his entire reason for being out in these fucking woods.

He hadn't trekked out into the wilderness to lose to Schmitt.

Pulling the SUV keys from his pocket, he handed them to Joy. "I'll cover you. Get in and get out of here. You got a radio? Call in backup."

"There's no backup. I'm the only ranger on duty for this entire section of park."

"One ranger? One fucking ranger?"

"Budget cuts," she said with a shrug.

"Fucking budget cuts." He shook his head. "Okay, just get out of here. Somewhere safe. Call the cops."

Not that the cops would get here fast enough to do anything. Part of the reason Howards claimed he used this particular rest stop. No law enforcement around for miles to complicate things.

"You said there were at least five people out there. They all have guns. I'm not leaving you behind on your own."

He had to admire her bravery. But he could do without the witness.

Another round of gunshots. Closer now. On the side of the building where his SUV was parked.

"Too late now." Damn it.

There was nowhere to run that wasn't right out in the open. And Schmitt and his people were closing in.

Another few shots, these from the opposite direction. The woods in that direction were farther away, too far to reach them at the bathroom, but it meant running in that direction would be running right into range.

"They're encircling us," Joy said.

"Yup." No time left to make a run for it.

A loud bang from behind the building made Joy jump. "What the hell was that?"

He had no idea. "Maybe they blew out a tire on the SUV?"

Moose hollered again. How the big guy hadn't been shot by now…

Another few shots, these from closer, and angled to hit the side of the building beside Connor.

Joy grabbed his collar. "Come on."

He stumbled after her as she dove into the women's bathroom and slammed the solid metal door shut.

3

"Don't suppose you've got a key to that lock?" Connor hunted the stalls, looking for something to block the door with.

"Won't hold for long," Ranger Joy said.

But it was something. The longer they could stall, the better chance he had of finding a way out of this mess. He also needed to get into the bathroom behind this one. He looked up over the stalls.

Blinked. Cursed.

There was a narrow gap in the bricks near the roof, a gap that meant the two bathrooms connected.

He pointed to the gap. "Bad for privacy," he said.

"Good for air circulation and keeping the smell down."

He supposed that was true. Still.

Would have been nice to know that was there before he wasted so much time trying to pick the world's worst fucking lock.

"We need to get into that side of the building."

"No way out," she warned.

"No way out no matter where we are in this brick box." First, he had to collect what he was here for. Then he could figure out how to get them out of this mess.

He stepped up onto one of the toilet seats. The gap between the roof and the wall was gonna be a tight squeeze, but there was enough room to slide through sideways.

He jumped down from the toilet seat and held his hand out. "Here, I'll boost you up."

Joy took his outstretched hand and jumped onto the toilet.

He looked at her hat. "That ain't gonna fit."

She took it off, squashed it flat, and slipped it through the gap. Then grabbing the edges, she pulled herself halfway up the wall in a show of upper body strength he had to admire. He got behind her, grabbed her legs and gave her an extra lift.

When the top of her body was through the gap, she swung her legs up and around, straddling the gap, her stomach on the narrow span of wall between the two bathrooms.

She looked back at him. "Can you do this without help?"

"Get down before the bullets start flying," he snapped. Questioning his upper body strength. Now that was just insulting.

She dropped into the other bathroom, her hands catching the wall. He heard a few curses and then she hissed, "Hurry!"

Yeah, he heard it too. Coming closer to the building. Voices.

Shit.

He stood on the toilet, grabbed the edge of the wall and pulled himself up, using the wall for foot purchase as he scrambled to get his leg through the gap. The whole thing was a lot more awkward and gangly than he would have liked, but he slipped through to the other bathroom minutes before a round of bullets hit the metal door on the side they'd just occupied.

Lifting his head enough to see the door over the ledge. No holes. Door still closed. Good. They had a few minutes maybe.

He dropped to the toilet beneath him, then stepped down.

This side of the building was so dark he could barely see and his night vision was pretty decent. The high windows—one of which was shot out thanks to Schmitt's people—let in a little ambient light from outside. But the other side of the building had been brighter. Light from the half moon hitting the windows there. No light leaked into this side, except past the gap they'd just dropped through.

He squeezed his eyes a few times, trying to adapt to the darkness faster. There was just enough light to see Joy's general shape, standing next to a pile of broken porcelain where the urinals would normally be. Plumbing pipes stuck out from the wall. And the smell was less than pleasant.

He wrinkled his nose. "This place needs an air freshener," he muttered.

Joy ignored his comment. "That door won't last long. And they're gonna figure out where we disappeared to sooner rather than later."

"Yup." He scanned the bathroom.

Sink. That was the place.

Barely visible in the darkness, little glints of light reflected off two metal sinks and a hammered metal mirror hung above them. Two lumps of pale plastic next to the sink were probably the dispensers for soap. And he could just make out a metal paper towel dispenser on the wall.

He searched around the base of the sinks, near the water pipe, feeling up to where it connected with the basin.

Cursed when he didn't find anything at the first sink.

"What are you looking for?" Joy whispered.

More noise from outside. Talking instead of gunfire. But the sound was too muffled for him to make out. Probably talking about how many ways they could kill him if they got ahold of him.

"We have to find a way out of here?" Joy said.

"Yup. Getting to that part. Just need to…" He felt along the second pipe, tempted to pull out his penlight, but he didn't want to risk anyone outside seeing the light.

He reached the basin. Nothing.

Fuck.

Howards had told him the flash drive was here. The sinks. He'd said the sinks.

Panic started to kick in. Without that flash drive, he had no way of negotiating with Schmitt. No way to talk him into letting Joy go.

He needed that fucking drive or he had no bargaining power.

He scanned the bathroom, the broken pits of porcelain, the two stalls like black closets, their doors ripped off and laying in a pile on the floor. He and Joy had climbed down into one of those stalls. But he hadn't checked them.

The darkness inside the stalls was almost absolute, though. When he poked his head inside one, he could barely see the toilet.

He was going to have to hunt with his hands.

He sighed. Dropped to his knees, and felt around the base and back of the toilet. It was also metal, cold, with no cistern. And it stank like it hadn't been flushed in a month.

Swallowing a rise of bile, he hunted the ground, the base of the toilet, the area behind the bowl where the pipes led into the wall. Nothing.

He scrambled around to the other stall, searching every bit of area he could reach.

Just as he started reciting one of his grandmother's curses, which he fully intended on using against Howards, his fingers brushed something.

Something hard, and small, and rectangular shaped. Taped to the very back of the toilet bowl.

Sink. Does this look like a sink to you, Howards?

He kept that rant to himself as he pulled the drive and tape from the toilet. Outside the stall, he held the drive up, trying to catch the faint light coming in through the gap.

All this for a little piece of metal and plastic.

And if he could actually get the drive back to Howards without dying, he'd get paid.

Never to return to the woods ever again.

"What is that?" Joy asked at his elbow.

"The thing that's going to get us out of here." He tucked the drive into his pants pocket and went to study the door.

"Bar lock, remember?" Joy said.

He nodded, his fingers working along the edge of the frame. And smiled.

Hinges. He could work with hinges.

He pulled out the little black, leather wrapped tool kit from inside one of the large inner pockets of his hoodie. The only thing he liked about sportswear were the pockets.

"How'd you know I was a city boy?" he whispered as he felt around the hinges a bit more, then pulled out the tool he needed.

"Your shoes," Joy said.

He glanced down, but in the dark, he couldn't see his black loafers. "I love these shoes."

"They're nice. They're just not for hiking."

That was a fair assessment.

"What are you doing?"

"Shh," he said.

The hinges were rough and he had to scrape off a little paint to get a good grip on them. But he managed to get the screw out of the bottom one without making too much noise.

Outside, everything had fallen silent. That wasn't good. Even Moose had stopped bellowing.

"Hope Moose is okay," he muttered as he went to work on the top hinge.

"They're hard to kill," Joy said, patting his arm.

The screw holding the top hinge in place came loose.

Just as something broke through the window in the other half of the building.

Connor hurried to the toilet and lifted up to see through the gap.

Smoke was filling up the bathroom.

4

"Time to go." He dropped to the ground and raced back to the door.

Joy wordlessly helped him lift the door up off the hinges. They pushed and shoved until they got the door free, pulling one side inward on the normally outward swinging door.

The main door lock and the connection to the bar lock kept the door half closed, so they couldn't drop it off completely, but they made enough of a gap to squeeze through and under the bar lock.

Connor went first, scanning the surroundings before slipping out and keeping the door pushed inward so Joy could wiggle through.

Schmitt's people had to be around the front, waiting for the smoke to force them back out of the bathroom. No one at this side of the building shooting at them anyway.

He grabbed Joy's hand because he didn't want to talk aloud. They hugged the building to reach the side where his rental was parked. The two back tires had been shot out.

They wouldn't get far on those.

Still better than standing in the open and getting riddled with bullets.

He edged toward the driver's side door, Joy just behind him, both of them crouched low so they weren't visible through the windows.

She followed his lead without question or argument. He was definitely starting to like her. Something about a competent woman.

He tried the car door. He'd locked it. It was still locked.

Joy handed him the keys she must have kept in her pocket. The minute he pressed the open button, this car was going to make noise. The people waiting on the other side of the bathroom were going to know something was wrong.

No help for it.

He hit the button.

Beep beep.

He winced, threw the door open and motioned Joy inside. She started to move…

A gun clicked.

Connor and Joy froze. He looked up.

Schmitt stood a few feet away. His gun pointed right at Connor.

First thing Connor noticed? Schmitt wasn't any more comfortable in the forest than he was. And he'd dressed even worse.

A suit. Tie. Pressed shirt. All in black, which made him hard to see in the dark. Just the flat silver color of his thick, long hair and his white goatee stood out in the otherwise meager moonlight. He was so fucking tall, when Connor blinked, it looked like Schmitt's head was hovering in the air without a body under it.

That was fucking creepy.

Schmitt smiled.

Connor really hated that smile.

"The flash drive," Schmitt said.

"I didn't find it. You can check. Wasn't in there. Just broken urinals and stench. I don't recommend the stench."

"Ha, ha. The flash drive."

Connor hesitated.

"The flash drive. Or we kill the ranger slowly instead of fast."

"I'd rather not be killed at all," Joy said.

"That's not an option now." Schmitt waved his gun at Connor. "Hand it over. Or you watch her suffer."

Joy gripped the back of his hoodie, her hands out of Schmitt's line of sight.

For a split second, Connor thought she was panicking, that she was looking for comfort with that gesture. Then he felt the bump of hard metal against his back.

Her gun.

Competence was extremely sexy.

"I didn't find it," Connor insisted, raising his hands. "I don't have it. You can search me if you want."

Schmitt considered him for a long moment, his expression thoughtful. "I could kill you and search you."

"You could," Connor said. "But then if I did find the flash drive and hid it again, you'd never know."

"You're lying to me."

"I lie a lot. You'll need to be more specific. To which lie are you referring?"

Schmitt cocked his gun. A showy, unnecessary move. But the threat was pretty clear.

"The flash drive, Connor. Now." He raised his gun.

"Okay, okay, look," Connor said. Then leaned to one side as Joy fired at Schmitt.

She hit him in the throat.

Connor blinked. He couldn't have made that shot if he'd practiced for months.

Schmitt gripped his throat, his face contorting. He raised his gun.

Connor grabbed Joy and dove into the SUV.

"Horrrnk!"

The sound of hooves hitting dirt was like thunder.

Connor pulled his legs into the SUV and slammed the door shut. Around the corner of the bathroom building, the rest of Schmitt's men came running.

Just as a whole bunch of moose came charging out of the trees.

In reality, it was probably only about three of them. But in the dark, it looked like dozens of them. They were so overwhelmingly large. Connor watched, eyes wide, as the moose ran right over the top of the men, despite them firing multiple shots at the charging beasts.

"Those bastards are as tall as the bathroom," he muttered. He'd swear their antlers were wider than his car.

"Don't mess with a moose. Definitely don't mess with more than one of them."

"I didn't know they charged." He couldn't look away. The bastards were *huge*. He'd thought Moose looked big face-to-face. This was just…

Terrifying.

Joy patted his hand. "It's okay, city boy. You get used to it."

Right.

They watched the chaos in silence. Two of Schmitt's men ran—the smart ones. One guy curled up into a ball as the moose stomped over him. Schmitt was lost to sight under the antler and hoof parade. At least one guy took the full force of a moose charging him with its head lowered and went flying back into the wall of the bathroom.

Connor winced.

"Ouch," Joy said.

"How long will they do this?" Connor asked.

"Until they've worked off their irritation." She crawled into the passenger seat of the SUV. "Wouldn't recommend stepping out there right now."

"What happens if they charge the SUV?"

"They'll knock us over and might kill us." She reholstered her gun and leaned back, watching the mayhem.

"Good to know."

"What's on that flash drive?"

"Financials. Incriminating stuff. I'm passing them on to law enforcement."

"You aren't law enforcement?"

"Not…precisely." He was a former thief and a current errand boy for the federal agent who'd kept him from a life sentence for a crime one of Connor's former victims had framed him for. But that was a little too complicated for a first meeting. He settled for, "Private contractor." As good a label as any.

After about ten minutes, the sound of pounding hooves and bellowing beasts subsided. He reached for the door handle, but Joy put a hand to his arm.

"Give them more time to clear out. We go out too soon, they'll charge again."

He settled back in his seat.

Joy nodded when the coast was clear, and they climbed out of the SUV at the same time.

He didn't look too closely at what the moose had done to Schmitt or the three others who hadn't managed to run away.

"Well that's unpleasant," Joy said. "Glad the moon's not full."

"Why?"

"Too much light."

Fair. "That was a good shot, by the way."

"Thanks. I've had a lot of practice."

"Shooting guys in the neck?"

"Target practice. First time I've shot a human."

"You okay with that?" He turned to see her face in the dim light. She was pale, but her expression was calm.

"I'll live with it."

He considered his SUV. "Can I get a lift back to somewhere civilized? Then we can call in the calvary to deal with…" He gestured at the bodies. "So long as you don't think the moose will eat them or anything."

"Moose won't. Wolves might."

"There are wolves in these woods."

"Cougars and bears, too."

"I hate nature."

"Wait'll I tell you about snakes and spiders."

"Shut up."

She smiled a little, some of the color coming back to her face. "Come on, city boy. Let's get you and that flash drive out of here."

They walked the long way around the bathroom to avoiding the bodies and moose mess.

Connor scanned the area as they moved across the open parking lot to her four-by-four, looking out for the men who'd run. No sign of them.

"You really working with the law, or are you conning me?" Joy said.

"What if I was conning you?" he asked, genuinely curious.

"I'd still get you back to civilization. But I'd give you a fake number."

"You assume I'm going to ask for your number?"

She smiled and climbed into her truck.

He smiled too.

He glanced back at the square cement brick building. The smoke bomb Schmitt's people had used on the women's side had dissipated. There were chunks of cement blown out of the bricks. Bunch of dents in the metal door. Someone was going to have a hell of a time explaining that mess.

He was just glad it wouldn't be him.

At the edge of the woods, just beyond the bathroom, he spotted the glimmer of eyes. A moose stepped away from the trees, far enough into the dim moonlight to show off his antlers. Then he snorted and turned back into the forest shadows.

Connor shook his head.

Who knew breaking into a fucking rest stop bathroom would result in all this.

What a night.

Thank You

Thanks for reading VACATION DEADLY! I hope you enjoyed the stories, got a few chuckles, and were able to escape to some fun settings. Although maybe not the rest stop bathroom Connor had to deal with.

As I mentioned in the Introduction, these stories fall right into some of my favorite fiction genres, but I only seem to commit action-adventure thriller every so often. One of those places is my book GALILEO'S PENDULUM, which is the start of an action-adventure series with a science history twist. If you prefer good old soft-boiled mysteries, you might enjoy my Percy James series, where the front desk clerk at a small boutique hotel in New York City gets the dubious pleasure of seeing a lot of weird stuff. And occasionally finds herself uncovering deeper mysteries.

Thank You

For more on my books and to keep up to date on my fiction, you can follow my website, check out my store, or follow my BookBub page or my author page at your favorite book vendor. I can occasionally be found on Instagram (mostly talking about baking and sports, but sometimes I talk about my books), or you can follow my Facebook Page.

If you'd like to know more about everything I write, you might consider joining my newsletter. Especially if you like action stories with a contemporary fantasy angle.

Thanks again for reading VACATION DEADLY!

Books By Kat Simons

About the Author

Award-winning author Kat Simons' debut action-adventure thriller, GALILEO'S PENDULUM, brings a mix of science history and fast-paced adventure to a little light forgery as her heroes race around the world to save an ancient relic. Her upcoming action-adventure mystery stories combine similar elements of adventure, world travel, and science—some of Kat's favorite topics.

She's also writing a soft-boiled, amateur sleuth series set in New York City. More known for being a popular hard-boiled mystery location, Kat wanted to show that even big cities can have small neighborhoods with a close-knit feel. From that idea, she started her Percy James series about the adventures and exploits of a front desk clerk working in a boutique hotel on the Upper East Side of Manhattan. Percy James sees a lot in that small hotel. And not all of it is legal. The series debuted with *Movies May Murder*.

After traveling the world, living in places like

Hawaii, Germany, and Ireland, where she got her Ph.D. in animal behavior, Kat now lives in New York City with her family and a library's worth of books.

For more on Kat and her future books

Website: https://www.katsimons.com/
Newsletter: https://bit.ly/KatSimonsNewsletter

KatSimonsBooks
https://tanddpublishingbookstore.com/

Social Media
Facebook Page: https://www.facebook.com/
KatSimonsAuthor
BookBub: https://www.bookbub.com/authors/kat-
simons
Instagram: https://www.instagram.com/isabokelly/

KATSIMONSBOOKS

For all Kat's books and book related merchandise!
Check out the store for early releases, sales, and fun!

https://tanddpublishingbookstore.com

Don't miss the latest Kat Simons
news, updates, excerpts, cover reveals, and more!
All new subscribers get two newsletter exclusive
stories.

Join Now!
https://bit.ly/KatSimonsNewsletter